*'The way I see it, y...
victim. A criminal...
It's my duty to pro...*

'This is ridiculous. Do you think I won't be missed? You can't just lock me up and think no one will notice.' Margo circled back to the crux of the matter. 'Keeping someone against their will is called kidnapping, Detective Archard, and that's illegal.'

He pulled a pair of handcuffs from his back pocket. 'Right now the best thing for you is plenty of bed rest.'

Margo's eyes widened. 'You wouldn't dare chain me to this bed like a dog, Ry. You wouldn't dare!'

'If you don't think so, then you don't know me as well as you think you do.'

Available in December 2003 from Silhouette Sensation

Protecting His Own
by Lindsay McKenna
(Morgan's Mercenaries)

The Prince's Wedding
by Justine Davis
(Romancing the Crown)

Once a Father
by Marie Ferrarella
(The Country Club)

Under Siege
by Catherine Mann
(Wingmen Warriors)

Bachelor in Blue Jeans
by Lauren Nichols

A Younger Woman
by Wendy Rosnau

A Younger Woman

WENDY ROSNAU

SILHOUETTE® SENSATION™

First published in Great Britain 2003
Silhouette Books, Eton House, 18-24 Paradise Road,
Richmond, Surrey TW9 1SR

© Wendy Rosnau 2001

ISBN 0 373 27144 1

18-1203

Printed and bound in Spain
by Litografia Rosés S.A., Barcelona

WENDY ROSNAU

lives on sixty secluded acres in the northwoods of Minnesota with her husband and their two energetic teenagers. A former hairdresser, she now divides her time between running the bookshop she and her husband opened in 1998, keeping one step ahead of her two crafty kids and writing romance. In her spare time she enjoys reading, painting and drawing, travelling and, most of all, spending time with those two crafty kids and their dad.

A great believer in the power of love and the words *never give up*, Wendy says that reaching her goal of becoming a published author is a testimony that dreams can and do come true. You can write to her at PO Box 441, Brainerd, Minnesota 56401, USA. For a personal reply send an SAE with return postage.

To my mom and dad
for always being there for me—
awesome job on the bookshelves and my table, Dad—
I love you.

To my father-in-law for his humour,
and to my mother-in-law for putting on wings
and rescuing me so often in my hour of need.

And always, to Jerry,
the rock that keeps me grounded,
and to Tyler and Jenni for knowing it all
and loving me anyway.

Chapter 1

Through the lens of her camera Margo zeroed in on the pier and brought into focus her brother, Blu, and the stranger. They were an odd pair, she decided, and wondered who the smart dresser was and what was so important that it required a meeting with the *Blu Devil* on a lonely pier at night.

They shook hands, ignoring the September rain soaking their clothes. The heavy mist gave the streetlights a distorted, eerie glow, making Margo's task harder. She was no master photographer, but Blu hadn't asked for a professional job, just visible proof that the *exchange* had taken place.

She hadn't asked what was being exchanged. Frankly, she didn't want to know. No, *this* wasn't about the right or wrong of anything. Her sole purpose for being in Algiers tonight instead of New Orleans behind the piano at the Toucan Lounge had nothing to do with morality and everything to do with sisterly love.

The night air had turned into a sponge, sharpening the odor of rotting fish and river decay. Margo wrinkled up her nose and swiped at her long, black hair. She could hear the constant slapping of the water against the boats tied dockside, feel the tropical air sucking her jeans closer to her slender, boyish hips.

Anxious to get out of the weather, she squinted through the camera lens and focused on Blu pulling something from his back pocket. Deciding this must be it, this was the *exchange,* she quickly clicked the shutter, then advanced the film. She had just raised the camera to take a second picture when a gunshot exploded out of the darkness. Frozen in motion, Margo watched in horror as the stranger jerked hard to the right, then crumpled at her brother's feet.

An involuntary scream climbed her throat, and she dropped the camera, vaguely aware that it shattered as it hit the asphalt. Mindless of the impending danger, she bolted from her hiding place and started to run toward the waterfront. As she reached the pier and climbed the steps, the pungent odor of cordite confirmed that she was now very much in the path of the melee. More shots erupted from somewhere behind her, and she nearly jumped out of her skin, crying out at the same time. Sheer panic overwhelmed her, but Margo's fear for her brother's safety overrode her fear for herself, and she forced herself to move forward.

As if the gunfire had opened up the sky and made the gods angry, a deluge of rain fed the sudden craziness. For a moment Margo thought the rain would be their salvation, and for one split second it was—

she slipped on the wet planking and went down hard. Seconds later, on her knees, a bullet whizzed past her head. She struggled back to her feet, her ears ringing, her knees bruised and throbbing. She searched out the spot where she'd last seen Blu, only to find he was no longer standing but sprawled on his back next to the unmoving stranger.

"No! Please, God, no!"

Margo's stomach convulsed. Fighting for air, she reached out and gripped the pier railing to keep from going over the side, her legs two disjointed pieces of rubber. She squeezed her eyes shut and began to pray fast and furiously, demanding that God hear her immediate need. When she was finished, over the pounding rain, she heard him. No, it wasn't God, but the voice was just as powerful, just as wonderful. She imagined the Almighty wouldn't have approved of her brother's choice of words, but Blu's deep voice scalding the air with profanity was sweet music to her ears—so much so that she began to cry.

Through happy tears, Margo watched Blu lift his dark head and lock gazes with her. A second later he was cussing again. *"Bon Dieu,* Chili! Get the hell off the pier! Are you nuts?"

His pet nickname for her made Margo cry harder—she and Blu had been so close growing up—so close in age and appearance that they had often been thought to be twins, though he was three years older.

A dark stain had spread over his left thigh, and Margo sucked in her breath, afraid of what it meant. She watched Blu roll to his stomach, his lightning-quick movements settling her worst fear—his wound couldn't be all that serious if he was able to move so effortlessly.

He swore at her again, this time in French, ordering her to dive into the water. Margo ignored the order. Number one, she hated water and had only learned to swim because Blu had dogged her for an entire summer the year she'd turned twelve. Two, her concern for him wouldn't allow her to abandon him. She wouldn't want to live if something happened to him.

She shoved away from the railing and started forward. She was almost there, almost able to reach out and touch him. Almost…

Two shots rang out in rapid succession. The first one whistled past Margo's ear, the one that followed made no noise at all.

She felt the bullet rip its way into her flesh, the force so intense, so staggering, it knocked her to her knees. The sharp pain stole her breath, then her balance. She swayed into the railing, felt the rough wood scrape hard against her cheek. Her knees finally buckled.

She heard Blu roar in protest, then he was beside her, gripping her arm and hauling her over the lifeless stranger. Still roaring in anger, he pushed her facedown into the sodden deck boards and threw himself on top of her.

Again crude language scorched the sultry night air, followed by, "I'll fry in hell for this if you die, so don't! You wouldn't want to send me to hell, would you, Chili? Keep breathing, *ma jolie!* Keep breathing, you hear?"

When he eased his weight off her to see if she was, in fact, still breathing, Margo muttered, "A few innocent pictures, my butt. What have you gotten us into? Who's shooting at us, Blu?''

"That's it, Chili. Get mad at me if it helps.''

His gaze shifted to the waterfront, and Margo followed her brother's gaze. Two men were climbing onto the pier, both carrying guns. Big guns. The kind seen in the movies. "Blu..."

"How bad are you hit?"

Margo grimaced as his hand passed over her blood-stained arm just below her shoulder. Ignoring her moan, he tore open her shirtsleeve to get a better look at the damage. "The bullet tore you up some, but the good news is you won't die." He flashed her one of his rare smiles, then glanced back to the two men who were advancing on them. "We're out of time. Come on, Chili.''

Margo glanced at her arm covered in blood. Her stomach rolled, and she briefly closed her eyes. "I'm going to be sick, Blu.''

"Not yet you're not. I'll hold your head like when we were kids, but later. Right now we've gotta go.''

"Go? Go where?'' Margo asked, sure she didn't want to know—Blu never did anything that didn't involve a certain amount of risk or skill.

"We're going swimming.''

"Oh, no! No! Not me.''

"Those guys, *ma petite,*'' he motioned to the duo closing in on them, then shoved something into the back pocket of her jeans, "they aren't headed this way to ask you for a date.''

"What did you put in my pocket?''

"The key to a treasure map. If I don't show up in a couple of days, give it to Brodie.''

"What are you saying?''

He leaned over and kissed her. "Just think of this as an adventure you can tell your children about some day."

There wasn't time to explore his ridiculous reply; he was already pulling her to her feet. Margo locked her knees like a stubborn donkey. "Blu, I don't like swimming, and you know how much I hate the river at night. I get my directions turned around and—"

"When we hit the water, swim for the *Nightwing*."

"You want me to swim all the way to River Bay?" Margo's eyes were huge, contemplating the half-mile-long swim to where Blu docked the fastest, most-talked-about cruiser on the river.

"Brodie's on board," he explained. "He's already heard the shots, so he'll know things have gone to hell. Have him take you somewhere where you can hide out for a few days."

"I can't go home?"

"No." He glanced down at her injured arm. "You need medical attention. I've got it," he said suddenly, "how about hiding out at the old man's place? No one would think to look for you there. *Oui*, it's perfect. He'll be able to take care of your arm, too. And I've changed my mind about the key. If I don't show up in a couple of days, give the key to him. He'll take it from there."

"You're crazy. I'd never go to him for help. Never! Not if I was penniless, or—"

A shot rang out.

Suddenly Margo was lifted half off her feet as Blu dragged her to the end of the pier. Then, they were jumping—jumping into the murky depths of the

Mississippi River while gunshots exploded around them.

"If you're there, God, get your scrawny backside out here." Ry craned his neck and scanned the dark alley in the French Quarter. In an attempt to escape the late-night rain, homeless bodies were huddled together on both sides of Pirate's Alley, their damp, unclean clothes giving off a ripe stench.

No one made an attempt to move or speak when Ry called out once more. Disappointed, he turned to leave, deciding that his snitch, Goddard Reese, had bedded down elsewhere for the night. Two steps into his departure a familiar voice brought him up short. "Just 'cause I ain't got no address don't mean I sleep denned up like a pack of rats."

God stepped from an alcove and into the rain. The minute he vacated the sheltered doorway, two ragged bodies leaped to their feet to crowd into the dry space.

Their intent clear, Goddard pulled his precious piece of cardboard from the doorway and tucked it beneath his arm. "Doan like sharin', neither," he grumbled, guarding his dry bed like a selfish child would his favorite toy. "You just get back from Algiers?"

Ry motioned to the dry alcove. "That's a prime spot. Choice accommodations like that usually require an early stakeout. If that's the case, and you've been here half the day waiting for sour weather, how do you know I've been across the river?"

Goddard grinned. "If I tell you all my secrets, Superman, you wouldn't need me anymore. I've grown partial to eatin' regularly."

Ry assessed Goddard's emaciated body. The man wasn't fifty years old, but his hunched shoulders and white hair easily added twenty years to his appearance. His cheeks were paper thin, his storm-cloud-gray eyes too small for his oversize, sunken sockets. It was true he ate at least once a day—thanks to Ry—still, the best snitch in New Orleans didn't weigh a hundred pounds.

"Talk is, one of yours ain't gonna get up with the sun tomorrow, Superman. Anybody I know?"

"You tell me. You're the one with ears in every corner of the city." Ry ignored the rain and settled his shoulder against the brick building. He was already soaked to the bone, his jeans hugging his lean hips, his shirt outlining his broad shoulders.

He'd spent the past three hours on DuBay Pier investigating the death of a fellow officer along with a crime lab technician, the coroner, plus a pile of uniformed patrolmen who had no reason to be there beyond curiosity. In the end, what he had was a dead cop with a hellish surprise burned into his eyes on a riddled pier; that and blood in three separate locations which suggested multiple victims. Only, there had been only one body: Mickey Burelly, a rookie cop who had come to the NOPD less than a year ago.

"I heard it was the suit they scraped off the pier," God said. "That yammerin' fool who liked to hear himself talk." The older man scratched at his chest, then dug deep into an armpit. "Guess he won't be worryin' about what color tie to wear tomorrow. Bet he wishes he'd've been movin' instead jawin', too."

How God knew what he knew always amazed Ry. But the point was, Goddard Reese, one of the many homeless in the French Quarter, had connections in places most people didn't even know existed. And he was right about Mickey Burelly; the kid did have a fetish for expensive suits, and he did like to *jaw,* as God put it. Maybe that's why everyone had ignored him when the kid had started crowing in the locker room yesterday about some big case he was about to crack wide open. Talk, as they say, was cheap. Every cop fantasized about *the* case, the one that would land him a notable raise, along with a front-page spread in the *New Orleans Times-Picayune.* The officers at the Eighth District were no different.

Goddard pulled up the collar on his ragged jacket and curled into the brick wall to avoid the rain. "If you ask me, that ain't the suit's style—holding a meeting in nasty weather. Hard on those expensive duds."

"Was that what he was doing, meeting a snitch?" Ry's ears perked up. As far as he knew, Mickey didn't have any solid connections on the street. Because he liked to talk too much no one trusted him.

"Don't know. Nobody I know worked for him. He was too stingy. He wore his money. Guess that didn't leave him any extra to work with."

Ry was always interested in Goddard's gut reaction. Like cops, the homeless who survived the gritty streets of New Orleans did so by their wit and intuition. God had lived in and around the Quarter longer than Ry had been a cop. At age thirty-three, Ry was about to celebrate his tenth year with the NOPD—the last two had been spent in homicide. Valuing God's street experience, he asked, "So what's your take on it?"

"Could be turncoat." God peeled his stocking cap off his narrow head and scratched at the thin strands on top. "Plenty of them around. More likely, some gutless wantin' a piece of somebody else's action. Fools everywhere these days. They find out, too late, they don't have big enough balls, and then you go to work scrapin' 'um off a lonely pier in the middle of the night."

Goddard spoke the truth. There was always someone willing to risk it all on a get-rich-quick scheme. But Mickey Burelly? Was there a chance he'd become an unwanted liability? Was he a dirty cop or had he been telling the truth yesterday when he'd been boasting about cracking open *the* case?

"I need a pair of eyes and ears for a few days." Ry pointed to the sign overhead. "Feel like sealing the deal with a plate of shrimp and a few beers? The Toucan serves all night."

"Now you're talkin', Superman." God offered Ry a toothless grin, then ducked back into the alley. Sidestepping the homeless vagrants snoring in each another's faces, he led the way to the Toucan's back door.

The hardy aroma of bisque and spicy crawfish teased their palates as the two men stepped inside the lounge. While large fans moved the rich scent into the dark corners of the dining room, the dim lighting and exotic decor set the mood for an evening of some of the best food and entertainment in the French Quarter.

As Goddard scanned the booths along the south wall, he asked in a hushed tone, "We gonna meet tomorrow?"

"You already planning your noon meal?" Ry teased.

The older man looked at Ry and grinned. "Tony's Thursday special is gumbo. All-you-can-eat gumbo. I like gumbo."

"All right," Ry agreed. "See what you can come up with between now and then, and I'll see you around noon."

Goddard spotted an empty booth half-hidden by a potted palm, and without any further conversation, shuffled his bird-like legs across the red brick floor.

Ry watched his snitch wedge the cardboard bed into the foot space beneath the table, then sit down on the purple-and-green leather seat. Seconds later, he reached for the menu.

The smell of steamed shrimp stirred his own hunger, but instead of finding his usual table, Ry took stock of his surroundings—more specifically, the small stage where Margo duFray sang five nights out of seven. The stage was dark, and that both surprised and disappointed him.

"Hey, *mon ami*, it's Wednesday. You got your days mixed up, no?"

The voice calling to him from behind the bar drew Ry's attention, and he turned to face the Toucan's owner. "I know what day it is, Tony."

"Then you're workin', *oui?*"

"That's right."

"Nasty night for it."

"Is the grill still on?" Ry asked.

"Yeah, sure." The big black man motioned to Ry's wet shirt. "If you don't mind me sayin' so, you've looked better. You oughtta go home and dry out with a bottle of cha-cha. Maybe curl up with somethin' soft.''

Tony's suggestion sounded good, at least the drying-out part, but Ry didn't need or want the distraction of booze or an easy woman. Booze had never been able to do the job it promised where he was concerned, and he had no interest in an easy woman whose name he wouldn't remember in the morning.

"What's that partner of yours doing these days?" Tony's grin fed the mischief in his heavy-lidded chocolate eyes.

"You know damn well what he's doing," Ry grumbled. "Not a damn thing."

"I guess I heard somethin' about that. Words between him and Chief Blais, somebody said. Suspended for two weeks, right?" Tony's grin opened up.

Ry shook his head. "You'd think by now Jackson would know to keep his opinions to himself. He's been suspended three times in the past year."

"You ain't turned your back on him, though. The two before you quit the first time Jackson said somethin' they didn't like."

That was understandable. Jackson had a knack for irritating the hell out of people, saying what he damn well pleased any old time he felt like it. But on the other side of that coin was the fact that Jackson was the best damn cop Ry had ever worked with. He was the fastest thinker, the sharpest marksman, and downright ugly mean when it was called for. No, contrary to rumor, Jackson Ward was the man every cop wanted watching his back, whether they knew it or not.

"You hear about the suit? Got himself kilt to-night."

Ry nodded without answering.

Tony leaned close and whispered. "That's why you're here, right? You're on the case, ain'tcha?"

"Looks like it." Ry ran a tired hand through his cropped sandy-brown hair, scattering rain drops, then hitched his jeans-clad backside on a barstool. "What's hot and ready, Tony? I haven't eaten since breakfast."

"Catfish in ten. Shrimp in five." Tony nodded toward a booth in the far corner. "Charmaine in two, if'n that look she's givin' the back of your head means what I think it do. She could dry you out real fast, *mon ami.*"

Ry curled his long legs around the metal rungs on the stool and glanced over his shoulder. Sure enough, there was Char running her pink tongue around the rim of her wineglass and watching him with those electric-green eyes that promised trouble. In no mood to baby-sit the judge's daughter, Ry turned back to Tony. "I'll take the safe bet, give me the shrimp and a cold beer."

Tony chuckled, his sharp eyes shifting to where Goddard sat clutching the menu. "You payin' for God?"

"That's right. Whatever he wants. As much as he wants," Ry added.

Tony flagged one of his waitresses to wait on Goddard, then turned to his grill and the shrimp Ry had ordered.

In a matter of minutes the familiar scent of gardenias drifted across the bar. Ry turned his head in time to watch Charmaine Stewart hoist her curvy hip onto the high barstool next to him. She looked as good as always, dressed fit to kill, out spending her daddy's money on trouble and anything else she could find. "I heard there was a shooting in Algiers tonight," she purred. "Need an ear? I'm a real good listener."

Ry dug into his pocket looking for a cigarette, then remembered he was out. Swearing, he said, "Why do shrinks and women always assume talking about your problems solves anything?"

"If you're not interested in talking, we don't have to. I'm good at other things, too."

Ry knew what she was good at—causing grief for her daddy. "I came here to eat, Char. That's all."

"Ouch. Aren't we in a nasty mood tonight?" She smiled, not at all daunted. "Come on, Ry, I'm a sure thing, and I know I could improve your mood. Say yes—" she paused, her frosty lips parting "—say yes, then take me home with you."

She had one of those refined Southern accents, the kind that easily attracted men. And Char had attracted plenty—the primary reason the judge was taking ulcer medication and seeing a shrink twice a week, Ry determined. "Shouldn't you be home? Your daddy—"

"Thinks you're wonderful." She reached out and ran a manicured finger over the back of his hand where it rested on the bar. "For the first time in just ever, Daddy and I agree on something." She giggled and leaned close. "You're our favorite detective, Detective Archard."

What she said about the judge approving of him was true enough. But Ry also knew there was a simple explanation behind that approval—if Char was seeing a big bad cop, the rest of the men making a nuisance of themselves might think twice. Judge Stewart was a shrewd old Creole. Ry didn't blame him for scheming to keep his wild, scandal-seeking daughter out of the newspaper. Only, he had no intentions of being her baby-sitter or anything else. They had already settled that months ago.

Char ran her finger further up Ry's arm. "You look like you've lost your dog and best friend all in one night. I can be anything you want, Ry. A lap dog suits me fine. You can stroke me or I'll stroke you. You name the game and I'm willing to play."

"You're wrong, as usual, Char. Tonight all I need is a hot meal and a few extra hours of sleep."

At Ry's mention of food, Tony came to the rescue with a plate of shrimp and a tall beer. "There you go, *mon ami*. Seconds are on the house. Jus' holler."

Ry shed Char's warm touch and picked up the fork next to his plate. He stabbed a plump shrimp, shoved it into his mouth and chewed vigorously. Unwilling to be ignored, she inched closer. "Remember the night I slipped through that hole in your hedge and found you asleep in that big hammock on your veranda? Remember how I woke you? The day's heat was nothing like what we sparked, and nothing has compared since, I'm not ashamed to say."

"Remembering that night doesn't do either of us any good," Ry drawled, reminded that when she'd arrived that night he'd been deep into one of his favorite dreams, a dream so potent and real that he'd almost made love to Charmaine Stewart thinking she was someone else.

She leaned closer and whispered in his ear. "If

you're tired I'll do all the work. Promise and—''
slowly she traced an invisible *X* across her chest
with a hot-pink manicured nail ''—cross my heart.''

Ry didn't doubt Char would be good at her word,
she'd had enough practice. His gaze drifted to her
full breasts, then lower to the rounded curve of her
hips beneath her pink silk T-shirt dress. A man
would have to be crazy not to take what she was
offering.

He stood, dug two twenties out of his back pocket
and laid them on the bar beside his half-eaten food.
Out of habit, he glanced toward the stage where the
piano sat idle. He still thought it odd Margo wasn't
there. A creature of habit, she was as dependable as
she was loyal. The only thing that would make her
take a night off was if she was sick.

Ry's gaze went back to Char. ''Want me to call
you a cab?''

''I take it that means you're turning me down
again.'' She wrinkled her nose. ''You're a stubborn
man, Detective Archard. But, lucky for you, so am
I.''

It was still raining when Ry left the Toucan and
turned his green Blazer toward the Garden District,
and his thoughts back to the Burelly case. It went
without saying he was committed to finding
Mickey's killer. Even though there wasn't much to
go on at the moment, the crime hadn't been perfect.
Along with Mickey's body, he'd found evidence
that someone else, possibly two other people, had
been with Mickey at the time of the shooting. A
blood trail leading to the end of the pier suggested
that they had attempted to escape by jumping into
the river.

Would the Harbor Patrol find their bodies in the next few days? Or had their escape been successful? The odds were slim that, wounded and fighting the river's current at night, a person could survive. That is, unless their wounds weren't serious and they were good swimmers who knew the area. Ry had learned that a slim chance was better than none. Until he explored every possibility, he would assume there were witnesses out there who could shed some light on his case.

He punched in the cigarette lighter, again recalling Mickey boasting about getting his picture on the front page of the newspaper. Well, he was going to make the front page, all right. Cursing the waste, then reminded that he was out of cigarettes once the lighter popped, Ry gunned the engine and sped past the Lafayette Cemetery. As he turned onto Chestnut Street, the red brick two-story came into view, and he hit the remote and watched the lacy iron gate open.

The rain had diminished to a fine sheeting mist, Ry noted as he killed the engine and climbed out of his Blazer. As he walked toward the rear entrance of the house, he could smell the night-blooming jasmine that grew tight to the veranda. He walked past a towering oak dripping with Spanish moss and strolled up the concrete steps. The iron railing felt warm to the touch—the day's incessant heat still evident after midnight.

On the veranda Ry passed by the rope hammock, gave it a push, then opened the back door that he never bothered to lock.

Back in Texas the ranch house had always been left open to friends and neighbors, the coffeepot full and hot, along with a radio playing as a form of welcome. When Ry had moved to New Orleans, he had promised himself that once he'd gotten his own home he would keep the same tradition alive. And though no one ever came around much except for Jackson, he'd kept his promise.

Inside, he switched on the light, then pulled his sodden blue shirt from his jeans and tossed it over a chair at the kitchen table. The tape playing softly in the boom box was a blend of flute and guitar, a Native American arrangement that fit his somber mood as well as his Texas roots. He left it on and turned off the automatic coffeemaker and emptied the two inches in the bottom. Efficiently he prepared tomorrow's brew, reset the timer, then turned the light off and left the kitchen.

A stairway just before the living room led to the second story. Tired, anxious to get some sleep, Ry climbed the steps, loosening his belt to remove his .38 Special from the compact holster tucked into the small of his back. At the top of the stairs, he turned left once more and stepped into the bathroom, his hand finding the wall switch a second later.

"What the hell!"

Ry quickly flipped off the safety of his .38 as he surveyed the room. There was blood in the sink and bloody fingerprints on the mirror. The closet door stood open. A small trail of blood led to the shower.

He eased into the room, checked behind the door, then warily crept to the shower and shoved open the slider. The white marble shower stood empty except for a white towel stained red that lay next to the drain.

Back in the hall, aided by the glow from the bathroom light, Ry took inventory of his surroundings. His closed bedroom door drew his attention and he arched a knowing brow—he never bothered to close doors in his house. Why should he? He lived alone.

The floorboards beneath his boots barely creaked as he took his position outside his bedroom. Then, silently counting to three, going in low and fast, Ry burst into the room.

The door hit the wall with a resounding boom, and in one fluid motion he flicked on the overhead light switch, then did a fast spin-around on his boot heels—his gun-hand outstretched, ready for whatever moved.

The force of the door smacking the wall brought the sleeping beauty lying on his bed awake. She jerked upright, at the same time her eyes went wide—familiar velvet-brown eyes that complemented sleek black hair and a pair of overripe, full lips. Ry's heart slammed against his chest as he remembered what it felt like to kiss those lips, how he had loved running his fingers through all that thick silky hair. Not wanting to go there, he quickly drove the memory out of his head and focused on the blood-stained towel wrapped around Margo duFray's arm.

Before he could speak, she said, "This isn't the usual way to ask a favor, I'm aware of that, Ry, but under the circumstances…" Her words stalled. She rested her back against his mahogany headboard. "I know what you're thinking. I know I swore I'd never ask anything of you ever again. They say you should never say never, and now I know why."

She looked beautiful as ever. Her voice a bit

shaky, but her chin was up, which meant whatever had happened to her hadn't gotten the best of her.

"Say something, Ry. You know I was never any good at reading your thoughts. You've always been more complicated than yeast. I'm a simple girl, remember? And right now, simple is all I can handle. So answer me, dammit. Have I humbled myself for nothing? You wouldn't turn me away. Or would you?"

Chapter 2

"What the hell happened, Margo? There's blood everywhere in the bathroom."

She had been waiting for him to speak. Now that he had, Margo hardly recognized the man behind the volatile voice. Louder than normal, with a biting edge to it, this was in no way the cool, collected detective she'd known a few years ago.

"Does that black look mean you're going to turn me out into the street, Detective Archard?"

"Cut the detective crap." He disengaged his gun, and in four long strides stood next to the bed, his jaw set as hard as granite.

Margo ignored the intimidation and braced herself against the headboard. She didn't want to reveal the degree of pain she was in—her pride stung enough, having given in to Blu's suggestion to show up on Ry's doorstep had taken every ounce of courage she owned.

Somehow she'd made it to the *Nightwing* after she and Blu had jumped off the pier, but what had happened after that was pretty much a blur. All she remembered was Brodie hauling her into the boat, then swearing crudely the minute he laid eyes on her arm. Seconds later they were on the move, the *Nightwing* flying across the river to New Orleans as if it had grown wings.

Margo's gaze drifted over Ry's handsome face. She had always loved looking at him—appreciated the mix of both hard and soft features sculpted over leather-tough Texas skin. He had the bluest eyes of anyone she knew, and the intensity of those magnetic eyes and his rich smoky drawl were a deadly combination. Never mind that his drawl wasn't as smoky just now, or his eyes as gentle as they could be.

She flinched as he sat down beside her. "The blood in the bathroom suggests this is more than a scratch, Margo. I need to see what we're dealing with."

"Sorry about the mess in your bathroom. I thought I could doctor myself. When I almost passed out, I gave up and went looking for a bed."

"You were never any good at dealing with blood, especially your own. How did you get here?"

Margo hesitated, not sure what to say.

He looked up. "Margo? Who brought you here?"

"No one," she lied. "I...I took a cab." She broke eye contact, feeling uncomfortable under his intense gaze. Absently she studied the generous bedroom decorated in navy and yellow. She'd heard he had moved into a house of his own, but it hadn't registered just how nice a place until Brodie had delivered her to the two-story Creole cottage in the Garden District. The rumor she'd heard of him selling his share of the family ranch back in Texas must have been true. It would certainly explain the influx of money that would allow him such a beautiful home.

"I'm going to remove the towel now," he told her.

His tone had softened, reminding Margo of the old days. His touch, too, brought back memories she had worked hard to forget. To someone who knew the history she and Ry shared, it would seem unlikely that she would seek refuge in his home. But Blu's idea had been ingenious. Well, she hadn't thought so at first, but later, when she'd had time to consider the few options left open to her, she'd had to agree with her brother. Who would ever think to look for her in the home of one of the most respected homicide detectives in the city of New Orleans?

And they *were* looking for her. Brodie had pointed to several spotlights combing the river as they fled Algiers.

It had been more than four hours since she'd slipped into Ry's house like a thief, squeezing through a hole in the hedge Brodie had stumbled on. Once she was standing at the door, supported against the iron railing that wrapped a wide veranda on all sides of his home, she'd urged Brodie to go back to the *Nightwing* and search for Blu. Of course he hadn't wanted to leave her, but they both knew Blu needed him at that moment more than she did.

Left alone Margo had taken a deep breath and knocked on Ry's back door. When he didn't answer,

desperation had forced her to try the door. Relief
had rushed through her veins on finding it unlocked,
and she'd crept inside like Goldilocks, all wide-eyed
and cautious. And then surprised and impressed
shortly thereafter—Ry's home was any woman's
dream come true.

"Why the hell didn't you say you'd been shot?"

Margo expected a reaction of some kind. She
hadn't been so foolish as to think she could pass a
gunshot wound off for anything else but what it was.
"That's very good detective work, Ry. You certainly know your job."

Her sarcasm wasn't appreciated. He swore, offered her a black look, then turned his attention back
to her arm. She felt him probe the wound, and she
sucked in her breath and held it. She wouldn't moan,
she promised herself, and she wouldn't cry out, either.

"You're lucky," he sighed a moment later. "The
bullet missed the bone. The excessive bleeding is
caused by a flap of skin that needs to be stitched."

Margo had already gotten a damage report from
Brodie. She would have let him patch her up before
she got to Ry's, only, for a big, tough fisherman,
Brodie had as weak a stomach as she did when it
came to blood.

Ry leaned closer, eyeing the scratch on her cheek.
To Margo's surprise she realized he still used the
same unpretentious cologne she had associated with
him years ago. Everything was familiar. He still
wore his hair short and carefree for ease's sake.
Even his day-old scruffy jaw was typical. She remembered how he used to complain about how

much time it took to scrape off his healthy growth of whiskers.

She should hate him, and most days that's what kept her going—the outrage and the humiliation and the determination to rise above it. Ry had not only crushed her spirit and scarred her heart, but he'd done it in such a manner that she had looked like a naive little fool. Of course he hadn't wanted a permanent relationship. What had she expected two years ago, marriage? He was older than her by twelve years. What man at age thirty-one would want to marry a nineteen-year-old, starry-eyed girl?

Oh, she hadn't wanted to believe that she'd been used, or that she'd been that much of a fool. But it was the truth—Ryland Archard had enjoyed the chase and the victory prize in the end, but he had had no intentions of sticking around for anything more—least of all a permanent relationship. She should have recognized the type—after all he was now thirty-three and still single.

Margo wanted to tell him he looked old and haggard. She would like to make a snide comment in reference to a soft belly or a sudden receding hairline. Only there were no visible signs that he had aged. In fact, Ry Archard, much to Margo's annoyance, had improved over the past two years much like a superior bottle of Chardonnay.

Then, too, she supposed needling him right now wouldn't be very smart. She was in his home, asking for his help. If she'd learned anything in her twenty-one years it was when to run, when to stand and fight, and, most important, when to keep her private thoughts private and her mouth shut. Tonight, the third applied without question.

"Come on, I'll help you up."

"Up? Why would I want to get up?"

"Because I'm taking you to Charity Hospital."

Margo's eyes widened. She had no intention of going to the hospital. Gunshot wounds had to be reported. There would be a dozen questions to answer; a report would be filed. And what if the men chasing Blu were checking out the hospitals?

"No doctor. I won't go!"

The quicksilver change in his eyes told Margo her hasty words had triggered his suspicion. "Why no doctor, Margo?"

She didn't answer.

"Come on, baby. Why no doctor?"

Margo cleared her throat, and this time she was careful with her tone, as well as her choice of words. "I hate men in white coats, that's why. They smell too clean and smile too much when there's nothing to smile about. I don't feel like playing twenty questions, either. The man who shot me is long gone by now."

"Tell me about him." It wasn't a request, but a solid demand.

Margo raised her chin. "I didn't get a good look at him. He wore an oversize hat that hid his face. I shouldn't have fought with him. I know that now, but when I saw the gun I just reacted. I've been walking home every night since I started working at the Toucan. I guess a year without a confrontation made me careless."

"So you were attacked? Mugged?"

"Yes." Margo slipped into the lie easily. As often as Blu had schooled her in the art of swimming and fishing, he had lectured her on the value of a fail-safe lie. That didn't mean she enjoyed lying, or that she did it on a regular basis. But she was confident that, in the right situation, she could keep her eyes from blinking and her voice rock steady while she attempted to cheat the truth. "He wanted my purse. Ah...my money."

"Where did this happen?"

"Near my apartment."

"One block? Two?"

"Does it matter?"

He raised his thick brows. "You worked tonight, right?"

Margo hesitated. Ry hung out at the Toucan on Tuesdays, Thursdays and Saturdays. This was Wednesday. Feeling confident, she said, "Yes, I just said so, didn't I?"

He stared at her a long minute. "So this happened walking home from work around ten?"

"Are you losing your hearing? I just told you that."

He ignored her smart remark. "So it was ten o'clock when you left work?"

Margo glanced at the clock on the nightstand. Quickly calculating the hours, she said, "I guess so."

"And you were shot within fifteen minutes of leaving the Toucan? Or was it more like twenty-five? Could it have been forty minutes? Fifty?"

Annoyed by his relentless questions, Margo said, "I didn't get up, look at my watch and say, oh my, I've been mugged at 10:20."

"Was it 10:20?"

Margo rolled her eyes. "No, I think it was 10:23."

"Dammit, Margo, this is important!"

"I don't know the time, all right!" Margo's voice wasn't as loud as his, but just as angry.

"Well, then, what the hell *do* you know?"

"That I'm going to have a headache if you keep badgering me like I'm the criminal here."

He stood and buried his hands deep in the hip pockets of his jeans. He appeared almost telepathic, Margo thought, as he stared down at her. Did he know something she didn't? As quickly as she asked herself the question, she reminded herself to stick with her story. Ry couldn't disprove a word she'd said, not unless he knew for a fact that she'd asked for the night off. And he wouldn't know that unless he'd questioned Tony, which she was pretty certain he wouldn't do—Ry was no gentleman, but he had kept their brief affair quiet. The only people who knew about it were her own family members and a few close friends.

"Why didn't you call Blu? Or Hewitt?"

"Brodie?"

"Come on, Margo. I know you've been seeing him."

Margo didn't disagree. Let him think whatever he wanted to. She said, "I couldn't get a hold of either of them."

"But you tried?"

"Yes, I tried."

"You really need to move out of that damn neighborhood. It makes no sense you living in that dump and surrounding yourself with those kind of people."

It made perfect sense to Margo, and because it

did, she felt like arguing. "It's close to work, and 'those kind' of people are my kind of people."

"That's crap. You have a job, take a bath regularly and don't sleep with a bottle. I hardly think they're your kind of people. What you mean is, they're Blu's kind of people."

"The rent's cheap." Margo refused to let him win a single round. He had won far too much from her already.

"So the rumors are true, then. You're giving half of every dime you make to Blu so he can throw it away on that worthless fishing fleet your father left him."

"The fleet isn't worthless. How dare you call it that!" Furious, Margo fisted the bed with her good hand, then gritted her teeth as a sharp pain shot into her injured arm. Gasping for air, she said, "The fleet was my daddy's whole life. And Blu wants it to be his. One day it'll be back to being the best fleet on the Gulf. It was once, it can be again."

"Take it easy. You're going to start bleeding again."

Margo leaned back and rested her head on the headboard and closed her eyes.

"You should be more concerned with your own life. Your own future, not Blu's."

"My life's perfect."

"This is perfect?"

Margo opened her eyes. "This could have happened to anyone, anywhere in this city. Where have you been? The crime rate here is double to anywhere else, maybe triple. Now, are you going to sew me up or not?"

He made a rude snort, then crossed his arms over his bare chest. "That's the favor? Stitch you up?"

"I haven't asked anything of you. Nothing since..." The words lodged in Margo's throat. She tried again. "This isn't a whole lot worse than the time I got that fishhook in my leg. You cut the hook out and sewed me up, remember? Good as new, is what Mama said when she inspected the job you'd done. Don't pretend you can't sew me back together because I know different."

A long minute ticked by.

Margo jerked her chin up a notch higher. "Fix my arm good as new, old man. You owe me that much. And by most standards, I'd say you're getting off cheap."

He flinched at her none-too-subtle reference to the past, then promptly got mad. "This isn't some damn fishhook accident. Hell, you've been shot! Damn lucky to be alive by the looks of it! Another inch or two and—"

"When did you take up shouting?"

"What?"

"I thought you hated irrational behavior. Doesn't shouting and ranting fall into that category?"

"I never rant!"

"Never say never," Margo taunted. "Tonight I had to eat that word."

"You could have died!"

"If that's true, and you care even a smidgen, I'd think you would be willing to help me out."

"You're missing the point."

"No," Margo argued, "the point is, you owe me and I'm here to collect. Now are you going to be a bastard and deny me, or sew me up so I don't bleed all over this expensive comforter?''

He didn't move.

Loath to be reduced to pleading, Margo forced herself. "Ry, please. I don't have anywhere else to go. If I go to Mama's, she'll fly into a panic and start crying and praying both at the same time. She has high blood pressure now, and…'' She could see he was weakening. "I suppose I could pay to have it stitched up on the street. I never thought about that, and I know this guy on the waterfront who—''

"The hell you will!'' He raked both hands through his hair.

Margo curiously watched him start to pace back and forth at the foot of the massive bed. She had always admired Ry's ability to remain calm even in a crisis. Now she wondered what could have happened in the past two years to have changed that. This was not the same overconfident, almost cocky cop she'd known two years ago. No, this new up-tight version appeared to be more human, even a bit vulnerable. And damn him, more likeable than the old version—that is, if she didn't hate him so much.

She held her breath, watched him wear out the thick rug. Suddenly he stopped pacing and faced her. "It's going to hurt like a son of a—''

"Forewarned is—''

"Not worth a damn if it doesn't change the fact. In this case, it won't. You need a local anesthetic.''

"I won't whine and call you names, if that's what you're worried about,'' Margo promised.

"If I do this, I'm going to expect a detailed account of what really happened.'' His eyes drilled her. "What *really* happened, Margo? Not some damn story about a mugger in a hat bigger than his head.''

''It's the truth,'' she insisted.

He strode to the door, then turned back. ''Do I look stupid?''

No, he didn't look stupid. He looked big and strong, and dammit, as handsome as ever. Margo hated to admit that one very disturbing fact, but he was Texas tough and remarkably well built, and...

Margo's gaze slid down his impressive bare chest. Further. Never one to mince words, she said, ''No, Ry, you don't look stupid. You look painfully uncomfortable. Do I still affect you, then?''

Her blunt assessment of his aroused condition was met with a frustrated, crude one-liner. Then he was gone.

Feeling a little better, now that she'd definitely won round one, Margo slumped against the headboard. Moments later she heard cupboard doors banging across the hall, followed by several colorful adjectives. He was angry, there was no question about that, but not so much so that he wouldn't help her, and that's all that mattered at the moment.

As his tirade faded, Margo sighed then closed her eyes. The soft patter of rain outside the second-story window became too obvious to ignore, and she soon began to listen to its hypnotic rhythm. Unlike her neighborhood, Ry's was incredibly quiet. The tall hedge outside reminded her of a live castle wall with the power to shield and protect. There was no street noise, no glaring lights. Only an enormous amount of peace and quite.

Margo opened her eyes and glanced around the room. The dark navy color complemented the lemon-yellow in a way she hadn't expected. Blending a feminine elegance with a masculine touch was perfect for a master bedroom.

It was nothing like what she'd grown up with. Her life had been all about secondhand clothes and cramped space. Glancing at the door, making sure there was no one to witness her weakness, Margo ran her hand slowly over the richness of the expensive, fat navy-blue comforter.

Again she closed her eyes, enjoying the feel of the supersoft fabric. Guilt followed quickly, and, feeling a bit ridiculous for enjoying the finer things in life, especially at a time like this, she quickly turned her thoughts to Blu. Eyes still closed, she whispered, "Where are you? Did Brodie find you? Will you come for me tonight or in the morning?"

The dark pier flashed in her mind's eye. Margo heard the gunfire, and suddenly she could no longer hold back the tears. A man had died tonight. Blu was wounded and missing. She worried that his thigh injury was more serious than he'd led her to believe, that the gunfire that had followed them into the water had hit its mark once more. Blu had abandoned her so quickly once they'd plunged into the water that she hadn't had a chance to say anything to him. She'd heard a huge splash after he'd pointed her in the direction of the *Nightwing,* then more rapid gunfire.

It was almost as if he had purposely attracted the gunman's attention to give her time to get away. God, if that was true, what had it cost him?

Margo had just finished wiping the evidence of her tears from her cheeks when Ry stepped back into the room carrying a bowl of steaming water, with a towel tossed over his bare shoulder. A threaded needle rode between his straight, white teeth. She glanced at the bottle of whiskey tucked under his arm and promptly asked, ''Are you going to get me drunk?''

He placed the bowl of water next to the amber lamp on the nightstand, then set the bottle of whiskey and threaded needle next to it. ''You drunk and my fingers oiled.'' He eased his weight down on the bed beside her. ''We're going to have to get your shirt off. How do you want to do it?''

Their intimate past made a mockery of his question. Yet the thought of losing her shirt, exposing herself to a man who had made a fool out of her two years ago, made Margo feel insecure in both her body and her intelligence.

''Margo? Did you hear me?''

''I heard you, Ry, and I imagine one arm at a time makes the best sense. That is, unless you want to show me some new trick you've learned with your boot knife.''

''That smart mouth of yours is wearing thin, baby. It wouldn't take much to change my mind and make a phone call to Charity Hospital. Don't push me.''

The hospital threat was sobering. Margo realized Ry was wearing his mood about as close to the cuff as she was. She clamped her mouth shut and reached for the first button on her ruined denim shirt. The movement cost her. A sharp pain shot down her injured arm, and she bit her lip to keep from crying out. She forced the first button through its hole, but the second one, much to her disgust, turned stubborn. After the third try, Ry brushed her hand aside. ''I'll do it.''

He unbuttoned the last three buttons quickly, his blunt-tipped fingers grazing her bare skin only briefly as he eased the fabric off her shoulder and down her injured arm. With gentle care he slid his free arm around her waist and drew her away from the headboard. As she rested against his solid chest, he whispered, "Easy, now. Let's take this real slow."

His warm breath teased Margo's ear, and suddenly all the pain and humiliation from the past came rushing back, along with an overwhelming amount of longing. She sucked in her breath at the same time a surge of poignant heat spread swiftly throughout her body. She knew it was normal to have some kind of reaction. After all, Ry had made her a woman, he'd been her teacher, her mentor— the man she had let strip her bare in body and soul.

But she'd also expected her anger would sustain her, that her pride would protect her. Now she realized it was too soon. Coming here, being this close to him, was the worst thing she could have done. It had been the mother of all dreadful mistakes, she realized, because as much as she wanted to deny it, the sudden desire she felt for this man was clearly branding her twice the fool. The feelings she'd desperately prayed would die were very much alive— a little tarnished and bruised, but still alive.

The rotten, disgusting truth was she was still vulnerable—vulnerable to his good looks, his voice, the musky scent of his skin. Every damn thing she had tried so hard to hate.

It was such a shock—like the resurrection of an old ghost—that Margo tried to pull free, refusing to be tortured and humiliated a minute longer.

"Margo?" Ry's arms loosened, but he didn't release her.

"I'm right here, Ry." Margo returned from her walk down memory lane, the sour taste in her mouth burning her throat and making her voice sound raw and husky. "I felt a little dizzy for a moment, is all. You can let go now."

"Not if you're dizzy. I can hold you a little longer, if that's what you need."

What she needed was for Blu and Brodie to suddenly appear and tell her this entire night was all a mistake. That the stranger on the pier was alive and that none of tonight was real.

He eased her back against the headboard, then tossed her ruined shirt to the floor. When she saw his eyes stray to her chest and the bloodstains covering her white satin bra, she said, "The least you could do is be subtle, Detective Archard. Ogling a woman when she's in need of help borders on disgusting."

He shrugged off her words and reached out to trace her bruised rib cage, then locked eyes with her again. "How did that happen?"

The injury to her ribs could be easily explained, but detailing how Blu had slammed her to the pier in order to keep her alive was out of the question. Margo brushed his hand away. "I don't remember."

"You don't bruise easy, Margo. I know that for a fact."

"I must have fallen."

"Must have?" When she didn't answer him further, he stood and strolled to the closet where he retrieved a clean shirt. As he came back to her, he said, "Do you want your jeans off before I get you drunk? I think it might be more comfortable sleeping in one of my shirts once you pass out.'' Without hesitation, he ripped the sleeves out of his shirt to accommodate her injured arm, not to mention the heat outside.

"Pass out?" Margo lifted one dramatic black eyebrow. "From the whiskey or the pain you're going to inflict on me with that needle?" She gave the needle a wary glance. "It looks awfully big Couldn't you have found something a little smaller?" She looked back and saw him smiling. It was the first time since he'd burst into the room wielding his gun that he'd allowed himself to relax.

"Second thoughts, baby?"

He was waiting for her to turn chicken, she decided. Feeling the need to win another round, she popped the snap on her jeans and slid the zipper down. She could feel his eyes hot on her, feel her own body feed off those damn unrelenting memories.

Determined to get through tonight no matter what, she asked, "You haven't acquired any kinky fixations I should know about before I pass out, have you, Detective Archard?"

Chapter 3

She had deliberately lied to him.

Oh, she hadn't lied about everything, Ry reasoned. She'd been shot, all right. But how and where still had to be determined. It certainly hadn't happened on her way home from the Toucan.

And the story she'd concocted about a mugger was no doubt a lie, as well. He'd seen plenty of gunshot wounds, and the bullet that had grazed Margo's arm hadn't come from a handgun a mugger would have pulled quickly and fired at point-blank range. No, Margo's wound had come from a larger caliber weapon, fired from a distance; he'd say at least thirty yards, give or take a foot or two.

That ruled out a face-off near her apartment. And to confirm that, no one had reported a disturbance—he'd called and checked after she'd fallen asleep. Then there was the lie about work. She hadn't been at the Toucan; he knew that to be true because he'd been there.

Ry's gaze slowly drifted over Margo asleep in his bed, her pale face pillowed in navy-blue satin. Where had she been tonight? It had been fairly quiet in the city, as quiet as it could be for New Orleans. But it hadn't been nearly as quiet across the river in Algiers.

The minute the thought entered his mind, Ry shook it off. No, Margo couldn't be mixed up in the shooting on DuBay Pier. But even as he dismissed the idea, he remembered how he'd found the crime scene—the way DuBay Pier had been riddled into sawdust by a high-powered gun, and his gut twisted a little tighter. Was it a coincidence that the pier wasn't far from the duFray Fish Market, owned and operated by Margo's mother? Or that Blu's fishing fleet was docked less then a mile away at River Bay?

Ry mulled over a dozen possibilities, then cursed out loud. So what if Mickey Burelly had stumbled onto *the* case of the century? And what if that case had involved Blu duFray?

Goddard had mentioned a turncoat, or someone possibly looking to make a fast buck. Everyone who knew Blu knew his financial situation. It wasn't news that the duFray Devils were struggling, doomed to go under at any moment. The repair bills alone on the aging boats were staggering. Knowing the way Margo felt about her brother, all Blu needed to do was give her a sad song and dance and her damn duFray loyalty would rise to the occasion.

Ry honestly believed Margo would risk her life for her brother if she found it necessary.

Had it been necessary tonight?

''Dammit!'' Ry focused on Margo's proud, beautiful face. She had been a curious teenager when he'd first laid eyes on her, and so beautiful it had hurt just to look at her. They had met by accident. He'd come upon her and an overeager boyfriend one night behind her parents' fish market—the boy testing his right to more than simply her company at the movies.

Ry had played the big bad cop that night. He'd chased the kid off, and promptly been swept away by the faultless beauty left standing in front of him all wide-eyed and obviously impressed by his white-knight antics. It had fed his ego—her admiration—and so it had begun, an older man's obsession with a teenager twelve years his junior.

For the next three years Ry had kept his distance, though he did see Margo from time to time at the duFray Fish Market helping out her mother. It had all started out so innocently, so he had wanted to believe. Only he knew it had never been innocent—from day one, he'd wanted her.

The night her father died, Ry found her weeping in the alley behind the fish market. He'd wanted to console her. He didn't even remember what he'd said, but suddenly she was in his arms, clinging to him as if he were her lifeline. And like a hungry old fox, he'd reveled in the fact that he had a legitimate reason to touch her and feel her body against his. She was jailbait; she'd just lost her father, dammit. What kind of bastard did that make him?

The guilt had driven him crazy, then it had driven him into the arms of another woman. He'd wanted Margo out of his head and out of his dreams; any woman would do as long as she made him forget his fantasy.

A year later he'd pulled over a carload of young people—the driver obviously intoxicated. He had motioned to the young man to get out of the car. When he did, Ry caught a glimpse of a shiny black head in the back seat. When he saw it was Margo something inside him snapped. He'd hauled her out of the car and into the squad so fast, the group of young people had fallen dead quiet.

On the way home she'd pleaded with him to let her out of the car. She hadn't been drinking, she promised, not at all—she wasn't going to go to jail, was she? He knew she hadn't been drinking, and he told her he was just taking her home. Relieved that he believed her, that she wasn't going to end up in jail, she'd leaned over and kissed his cheek. It had happened so fast, but just as fast he had pulled to the side of the rode and dragged her across the seat and kissed her the way he had always dreamed of kissing her. The next thing he knew, she was in his lap wrapping her arms around his neck offering him her hungry little mouth.

He'd done the math quickly. She was nineteen, no longer jailbait—no longer off-limits. And she was kissing him like she knew what she was doing.

He'd lost control after that, and before he had taken her home, they had stopped off at his apartment.

It had been the beginning of the end for them. A short month of heaven, and then hell had arrived in town and ripped their lives to shreds.

Ry's gaze locked on Margo's jeans where he'd tossed them to the foot of the bed. Immediately his body reacted to the memory of undressing her, stripping her long legs bare, exposing her slender thighs. If he was a man who believed in fate and happy-ever-after, he'd say Margo's sudden appearance in his bed after two long years meant something.

Swearing softly, Ry walked to the window that overlooked the backyard. It had stopped raining, the night air as heavy as a flannel blanket and twice as warm. He closed his eyes, tried to chase the sight of Margo's lithe body out of his head, but it was no use. Content to simply suffer, he relived each agonizing minute of easing her jeans down her narrow hips, then moved on to his fingertips brushing her satin panties, grazing her tanned, flat belly. And like he'd been doing for the past two years, he relived his own body going through its tortured ritual each and every time he allowed himself the pleasure of remembering how unbelievable that one incredible month with her had been.

The sound of her mumbling the word *cold* jerked Ry back to the present. Feeling the effects of the weather as well as his own physical frustration, he couldn't imagine how Margo could be cold. Nonetheless, a sheen of perspiration covering his bare chest, he left the room and found a blanket in the hall closet. On his return, he spread the covering gently over her, then left the room again.

While he paced the hall, he went over everything she'd told him. He played back phrases she'd used, dallied with the what-if game and ten minutes later he was back inside, shedding his boots and socks, prepared to spend a sleepless night in the stuffed chair he'd pulled close to the bed.

Halfway through the night she started to babble

incoherent phrases. Ry reached out and felt her forehead, expecting to find her burning up with a fever.
To his surprise and relief, she was cool. When the
babbling continued, he pulled the nightstand drawer
open and flipped the switch on a sophisticated three-
inch recorder. When she began to thrash and fight
the visions haunting her mind's eye, he leaned forward and placed his hand on her cheek. "Easy,
baby. You're safe with me."

Still caught up in whatever it was, torturing the
dark recesses of her mind, she cried out Blu's name.
And there it was. Ry's greatest fear had just been
realized—whatever dirty business Margo had fallen
into tonight had been prompted by her brother—and
he figured that could involve damn near anything,
knowing Blu the way he did.

Ry dozed off an hour later, something he had
fought hard against. How long he was out, he didn't
know. The sound of water running in the bathroom
jarred him awake, and he slammed himself upright,
his gaze locking immediately on the bed. When he
found it empty, he jumped to his feet and headed
for the open door.

The sight of Margo weaving slowly back into the
room hauled him up short. "You should have kicked
me awake if you needed something," he growled,
then hurried toward her.

She didn't say anything, just stood there with her
right arm drawn close to her side, her face ghostly
pale. Afraid she would fall, he lifted her into his
arms and carried her back to bed. As he carefully
laid her down on the soft mattress, he scolded, "No
more getting up without my help. You could have
fallen, dammit. If you break open those stitches, I'm

taking you to the hospital whether you like it or not.''

"You can try," she muttered, her voice half-strength.

He pulled the covers to her chin. "You still cold?"

"Cold?"

"You've been talking in your sleep." Ry noticed his words gave her pause. "What's the matter, Margo, you afraid you said something you shouldn't have?"

"No," she insisted.

Ry didn't press the issue, though he damn well wanted to. He would get the truth out of her. That was his job, and he was damn good at it. "Go back to sleep, baby. You need to rest."

She nodded, tried to get comfortable and winced in the process.

"I almost forgot, I've got some pills. I'll get you a couple." He started for the door, surprised that he had forgotten about the sleeping pill in the medicine cabinet.

"No pills."

Her objection stopped him and he turned around. "They won't hurt you. They'll just take the edge off," he promised, knowing that the prescription was potent as hell. A life saver when you needed to forget for a time and let sleep rescue you from your pain—pain of any kind; the pill didn't discriminate.

"I don't take pills."

"More whiskey, then?"

"So I can do more talking in my sleep?" There was accusation in her tone, in her beautiful brown eyes.

He strolled back to the bed. "Afraid you'll share your darkest secret with me? Afraid you'll confess you still love me?" The comment was ridiculous of course, but Ry had always hoped she still cared for him, that even after he'd played the bad guy, he hadn't destroyed everything they'd shared.

"I never loved you," she insisted. "I only thought I did. I guess that's what you get for robbing the cradle, Detective Archard—a girl too young to know her own mind."

"Did a shrink convince you of that?"

"A shrink?" She frowned. "Why would I need to go to a shrink?"

Ry passed off her question with a shrug, then sat on the chair. "I thought it was the thing to do these days. Everyone has a shrink, right?"

"For what it's worth, I think there are far too many shrinks out there advocating whining these days. They always say something stupid like, talk it out and you'll feel better. What they should be saying is, you're not the only one in misery's boat, so shut up and paddle through it."

Ry grinned, reminded of how refreshing he had always found Margo's honest assessment about anything she had an opinion on. "Go back to sleep, and next time you need to use the bathroom, wake me up so I can help you."

"So you can watch?"

Enjoying her sudden spunk, he teased, "A perk for rescuing you? I like the way you think, baby."

She eyed him without saying a word.

"Come on, Margo, backing down so soon?"

"We both know the truth about you, Detective Archard."

"And just what truth do you think *we* know?"

She hesitated only a few seconds before saying, "You taught me how to kiss dirty, old man? I was barely eighteen that first time."

She knew she'd been legal. But Ry had to agree she'd still been too young for a jaded cop who kept a .38 Special in the bread saver in the kitchen. But just for the record, he said, "You know you were nineteen plus."

She closed her eyes and muttered, "How long?"

"How long, what?"

"I met you when I was fifteen. How long had you wanted me?"

The question was unexpected. But she was right to imply it had been an on-going problem for years. He'd been crazy to have her, so crazy that when he had finally gotten her into his apartment that first time, he'd been a man on a single-minded mission. He wasn't proud of the fact that he had ached to have her, that he'd made love to her virgin body three times the first night before he'd come up for air. Back then his ego had been the size of his libido, full-blown and hungry to be stroked. And when she had met him more than halfway, nothing could have stopped him from climbing inside her except her objection. But that hadn't happened because she had confessed that night she had wanted him with the same crazy intensity.

But it hadn't been just her body that had held him prisoner, though he knew that's how it had looked at the time. Honestly, he'd fallen in love with the entire package; from her sexy smile to the way she combed her hair. He'd loved it all—her voice, her walk, the way she brushed her teeth.

And he had known from the beginning, and at the end, that his life had been made better by knowing her. That's why walking away had damn near killed him.

"That long, huh."

"Margo—" Ry paused "—maybe we shouldn't be talking about this."

"You're probably right. I'm with Brodie now and you're with… some blonde, I imagine. I read in *Cosmopolitan* that 75 percent of today's men have a blonde in their bed, one at the office and keep a spare in the trunk of their car."

"Margo—"

"Go away and let me sleep," she insisted, turning her head away from him and closing her eyes.

The next time Margo opened her eyes, the sun was shining through the long narrow windows draped in sheer panels of pale yellow. She blinked out of her sound sleep, her gaze going straight to the occupied chair, a big, round, tufted half-circle in a yellow paisley on navy-blue.

"Good morning."

Margo moaned and slowly pulled herself upward to lean against the headboard. Her head spun, her arm throbbed. She screwed up her face. "It feels like a dozen marbles are rolling around in my head."

"And your arm?"

"Like you cut it off with a razor blade."

"That's what happens when you get yourself shot, then drink whiskey like a fish in a drought."

"And this is something I volunteered for, right?"

Margo leaned her head against the headboard and closed her eyes.

"I'm not going to apologize for the booze. It got you through the night."

Margo opened her eyes, then her mouth, to offer a witty comeback. Thinking better of it, she fell silent and averted her eyes. She had already taken a quick inventory, noting that Ry was no longer bare above the waist. He looked refreshed and put together—no doubt he'd showered while she slept. He'd shaved, too. His clothes were a simple gray T-shirt and scruffy jeans. The rugged look suited him right down to his brown, street-scuffed Texas boots.

"I drank too much, too," he admitted. "I need some head pills. You, too, by the sounds of it."

Margo turned in time to see him grip the back of his neck and vigorously massage it. "I don't want any of your pills, thank you."

He stopped rubbing his neck and looked at her. "I've been shot before. The day after is the worst. Trust me, you need—"

"Trust *you?*" Margo sniffed and rolled her eyes heavenward. "I wouldn't trust you with my library card."

"What was that last night, then? I seem to remember you trusting me with a needle and thread. Drunk, no less."

"You were the only cop that owed me a favor," Margo reasoned. "I didn't want to worry Mama. I told you that."

He relaxed back in the chair and crossed his leg over his knee. "Still as stubborn as ever. Your mama always—"

"Complained about that flaw. Yes, I know. But where does she think I got it? She's twice as stubborn as my father ever was. And Blu... Well, he isn't exactly a docile kitten, now, is he?"

It had been a slip of the tongue to mention Blu. Margo saw Ry's jaw jerk, and she decided that his opinion of her brother hadn't changed. Ry still thought Blu was irresponsible and selfish. What he didn't know was that Blu thought much the same thing about him.

"Speaking of the Blu Devil, have you seen him lately?"

Margo shook her head. "No, not for a few days."

"He still docked at River Bay, living on the *Nightwing?*"

"You know he is, Ry. You were there a few weeks ago harassing him about some nonsense."

"I was just doing my job, Margo."

"I might be young, but I'm not stupid. You're a homicide detective, remember? You don't investigate assault charges."

"Okay, so I volunteered for that one. Blu's temper being what it is, most of the guys down at the precinct would prefer tangling with a copperbelly."

Margo brushed the covers aside and slid her long, bare legs over the side of the bed. "I would really like to stay and chat about my brother's faults with you, but I don't have time. Would you mind getting my clothes for me?"

"You think you're leaving?"

"I don't *think* I'm leaving, I *know* I'm leaving."

Last night Margo had made a decision to head back to the *Nightwing* if Blu hadn't rescued her from Ry's home first thing in the morning. Yes, this was the perfect place to hide—that is, if she could keep her mind off the past. But she'd been trying and it wasn't working. Staying here would be emotional suicide.

She saw Ry's stubborn jaw lock. "Well, you didn't think I was going to stay, did you?"

"Actually, I did. Most people take a few days to recuperate after being shot."

"And I will."

He stood. "You've got nine stitches in your arm. You live alone. Who's going to look out for you?"

"Brodie."

"But you can't reach him."

"I haven't tried yet today," Margo argued. "Now, I'm grateful for your doctoring skills, Ry. If I forgot to mention that, it was an oversight. But now I have to go. I'll call a cab, and—"

"Forget it. You're not leaving."

Margo inched her backside to the edge of the bed and stood. She didn't feel the best, but well enough to make it out the door. She hoped. "You can't keep me here against my will, Ry."

"Can't I? Look at you, you can hardly stand up straight. And since no one knows you're here I control the situation. The way I see it, you're a gunshot victim. A criminal is still at large. It's my duty to protect you."

"This is ridiculous. Do you think I won't be missed? If I don't show up for work tonight, or at least call, Tony will send someone out to look for me. I have friends and family who really care about me, you know. You can't just lock me up and think no one will notice." Margo circled back to the crux of the matter. "Keeping someone against their will is called kidnapping, Detective Archard, and that's illegal.''

He pulled a pair of handcuffs from his back pocket. ''Right now the best thing for you is plenty of bedrest.''

Margo's eyes widened. ''You wouldn't dare chain me to this bed like a dog, Ry. You wouldn't dare!''

''If you don't think so, then you don't know me as well as you think you do.''

Margo eyed the portable phone on the nightstand. ''I have a job. If I don't show up for work, Tony will fire me. He's already…'' She snapped her mouth shut, aware she was about to mention how unhappy he had been when she'd called and asked him for last night off.

''Tony's already what?''

''Nothing.''

''You're Tony's meal ticket. He's not going to fire you, not after the increase in business you've given him over the past year. You're the best thing that's happened to the Toucan, and everyone knows it. I'll have someone call and explain you're sick.''

Margo wanted to scream. Instead, she said, ''There is no reason I can't work tonight.''

''I've seen you perform, baby. Your act includes playing the piano. Damn hard one-handed. Not impossible but…'' He rattled the cuffs. ''Back in bed, or be prepared for what happens next.''

He couldn't do this to her. Furious, Margo shook her head. ''No!''

''The cuffs or a promise to stay inside my house until I get back. That's the deal, Margo. Choose.''

Again Margo eyed the phone, considering her options. Fine, she'd do as he said, and then once he left she would be on her way one way or another. She eased down on the bed and swung her legs back on the mattress. "I hate you."

"Say it. Swear to me you won't leave."

"You're a jerk, a creep and a sadistic—"

"Swear on your father's grave." He rattled the cuffs.

"I swear, okay!"

Satisfied, he stuffed the cuffs back in his pocket. "Hungry?"

"For a piece of your liver," Margo spat.

"Seriously, you need to eat something. What can I fix you?"

"You're going to cook for me? You can't cook, remember?"

"I've learned. At least I can get by until you can cook for me," he taunted. "How does that sound?"

Margo didn't bother to remind him she wasn't going to be around long enough for that. She simply sneered back with a honey-coated grin and said, "Do you have arsenic in the house?"

He chuckled. "No, but I have eggs and shrimp. Still like shrimp for breakfast?"

The question and the memory it manifested had Margo biting the inside of her cheek. The pain reminded her of how dangerous it was to reminisce, as well as how vulnerable it made her feel.

"With shallots and chives?" He added, twisting the knife a little deeper.

"Cook what you want," she snapped. "Start the kitchen on fire for all I care. Better yet, how about yourself?" Margo squeezed her eyes shut and pretended to tune him out. Suddenly she caught the scent of him, felt his hand on her forehead. Her eyes popped open. ''What are you doing?''

''Making sure you don't have a fever.''

When his hand left her forehead, he shoved it into his back pocket and pulled out a key. A twinge of panic knotted Margo's stomach. My God, she'd forgotten all about Blu's key.

''Recognize this?''

Margo clamped her mouth shut.

''Of course you do, it came from your pocket.'' He was no longer grinning, his blue eyes razor sharp as he held Blu's key up so she could see it clearly. ''After breakfast we'll discuss what it unlocks.''

He slipped the key back into his pocket, then reached for the portable phone on the nightstand and pocketed that, too. On his way out the door, he said, ''I almost forgot. There's a tape recorder in the drawer next to you. While you're waiting for breakfast why don't you listen to it?''

''I don't feel much like listening to music,'' Margo sniffed.

''It's not music, but it's just as entertaining. You don't sound like yourself, but you were in a lot of pain last night. Well, maybe it wasn't so much the pain as the whiskey talking, you think?''

He walked out of the room then, leaving Margo to wonder if the liquor he'd poured down her throat, had, in fact, done the dirty deed and loosened her tongue. And if that was the case, just what had she told Detective Archard that she shouldn't have?

Chapter 4

His instructions had been specific—no one was to die. Not until he'd gotten his shipment back, that is. And maybe not even then if there wasn't a good enough reason. Keeping a low profile, even in a city this size, had always been the key to his success and survival.

Why, then, had his wishes been ignored and the job bungled so badly? The answer was simple—it was impossible to find good help these days. More to the point, his cousins were idiots.

Swearing crudely, Taber Denoux lifted his glass of cognac to his lips and swallowed the expensive amber liquid. He'd just finished talking to his best customer, and the man was livid. His merchandise was missing, and Taber hadn't been able to promise a recovery date. Oh, he had promised the merchandise would turn up, but without a date, the customer had threatened to buy elsewhere.

Damn Blu duFray to hell, Taber thought. Was the man an idiot like Rudy and Raynard, or the very devil his name implied? A more important question was, how had a going-broke fisherman pulled off a heist worth millions?

Unable to believe his merchandise was gone, Taber slammed the empty glass down on his desk. Blu duFray was either damn lucky, or his fisherman guise was the perfect cover for a well-connected thief.

Taber still didn't know how the cop fit into the scheme of things. And he conceded that he might never know. But, what did it matter now? The cop was dead. It seemed the only thing that had gone right last night was Raynard shooting low and wounding Blu duFray instead of killing him along with the cop. duFray dead would have only magnified the problem, since it seemed he was the only one who knew where the missing merchandise was.

Taber silently admired the Blu Devil's brashness, as well as his daring escape. The river at night was treacherous—made worse if you were carrying around a bullet in your leg. But as much as he respected the man's tenacity, he still wanted duFray's neck wrung as soon as he had recovered his stolen goods.

Taber glanced around his immaculately furnished penthouse high above the city. Beautiful objects were his weakness, and he'd surrounded himself with expensive paintings and artwork fit for a king. His tastes were a bit eccentric, as was his own appearance—the long, blond hair he wore flowing past his shoulders a striking contrast to his shiny black suits. He resembled a twenty-five-year-old man. Not bad for a man nearly forty.

He slid from behind his polished white desk and ambled to the wall-to-wall window that overlooked the city of New Orleans.

The morning was sunny, the weather report promising another humid day in the nineties. Taber gazed down on the people below, amused by their small, insignificant lives in comparison to his own. They really were pitiful, he mused, watching them scatter like ants in a frenzy.

His thoughts returned to last night and the uncomfortable situation he now found himself in. Antos, his most dependable man, had mentioned a woman on the pier with duFray, that she had also been shot by his cousin, Raynard, but that she, too, had escaped. Taber admired bravery as much as he did loyalty—they were both hard to find in a man, let alone a woman.

Curious to know more about this woman, Taber strolled back to his desk and picked up the phone. When Antos answered, he said, "I want her found, the woman on the pier. I want her name, where she lives, and I want the information yesterday."

Before Antos had a chance to confirm the order, Taber hung up the phone. He splashed more cognac into his glass, then wandered back to the window. By rights, the woman was his enemy. Then again, hasty decisions were made by fools.

She wiped her pretty mouth on her napkin, then licked her lips. Ry stifled a moan and instead asked, "Did you listen to the tape?"

"What do you think?"

She motioned for him to take the breakfast tray balanced in her lap, the scrambled eggs and shrimp smothered in shallots and chives all gone. Ry reached for the tray and set it on the nightstand. "So explain to me again what you were running from?"

"I already told you, or have you forgotten how you found me last night?"

No, he hadn't forgotten. She had nearly given him a heart attack. For sure, she had shortened his life by at least five years. "There was a shooting in Algiers last night," he offered. "A cop was killed."

She sucked in a fast breath of air, then tried to cover it up by clearing her throat. "A cop? Was he a friend of yours?"

"He? I didn't mention the cop was male."

She hesitated only a split second. "I just assumed."

Ry circled back to an old question. "You said you worked last night. Was it busy?"

"Yes. The rain always draws a crowd."

It was a good answer, but not the answer Ry was looking for. "Can you prove you were there?"

"Will I have to?" When Ry didn't answer, she raised her chin and offered a breathy little sigh. "If I must, then I will."

He hadn't expected her to have an alibi. That meant she was sure Tony, and the others at work, would cover for her. What did that mean? Were they used to covering for her? Did she ask them to lie for her often? "So you're serious about Hewitt?" The question wasn't planned and it surprised Ry as much as it did Margo.

"Excuse me?"

"It's a straight question, Margo."

"But not very professional, Detective Archard."

Ry climbed out of the paisley chair and stuck his hands in his back pockets. "But a legitimate question. Standard in a situation like this. Is your relationship with Hewitt healthy? Do you ever argue? Do you know where he was last night?"

"Brodie had nothing to do with me being shot."

She settled her hands in her lap like a innocent child. Hell…Margo innocent? What was he thinking? She had stretched every boundary her mother had ever given her after her father had died, and he knew she'd done things her way long before that, too. "Answer the damn question, Margo. Are you sleeping with Brodie Hewitt?"

She took her sweet time answering. "Well, you know what they say. Once you've tasted sugar, it's hard to go without. Who are you sleeping with these days, Detective Archard? As I remember you used to have quite a sweet tooth."

Ry tried to keep from getting angry. It was natural for her to choose Hewitt, he supposed. People often fell back on what they knew and who they were comfortable with. After all, Brodie Hewitt had been working with Blu for the past three years, waiting patiently in the wings for Margo to notice him. The bastard.

Ry felt like chewing the heads off nails every time he thought about Margo with Hewitt. He wanted to strangle Margo and shoot Hewitt in both kneecaps. Worse, he wanted to make Hewitt disappear for good and had considered it a hundred times.

Dammit! He was losing sight of what was important here. And he was acting like a jealous jackass, to boot. Margo had just been shot. He should be basking in the knowledge that she hadn't been killed. Only, the baggage from the past was upsetting his standard routine. It was the remembering that was to blame. An ironic parallel, since it was the remembering that had kept him sane for the past two years.

"What about this key?" He dug it out of his pocket. "What does it open?"

"I've never seen that key before you showed it to me an hour ago."

Angry all over again, Ry reached out and wrapped his fingers around Margo's slender throat. "Don't play this game with me, baby. I want answers. Clear, simple, truthful answers. And I want them now!"

"Let go, Ry," she whispered through his choke hold.

"I can't help you if you don't trust me."

"Take your hands off me, Ry."

He did the opposite and squeezed tighter. "Were you on DuBay Pier last night? Are you mixed up with Mickey Burelly's murder? Tell me the truth, dammit, or I swear I'll—"

She reached up and pried his hand off her throat. "You'll what, choke me? Throw me in jail? No you won't. You'll demand and threaten, and when that doesn't work, you'll back off and come at me again from a new angle. But I'm telling you right now, I don't have any new story you want to hear. So why don't you save us both the frustration and let me get the hell out of here?"

Furious with her, Ry spun away from the bed. He had to get out of there, had to regain control; he hadn't intended to bring up the murder on DuBay

Pier. Not yet, anyway. He'd just been so damn angry at her for continuing to lie to him with such ease.

He stalked to the door, then turned back. "My new angle is this, baby. Until I'm convinced what happened to you last night has nothing to do with my case, you're my permanent houseguest."

"The murder on DuBay Pier is *your* case?"

"That's right. My case."

Her eyes went wide, and her mouth dropped open.

"That look says it all, baby. You should have thought about the consequences of coming here before you bled all over my towels and climbed into my bed." In three long strides Ry was back at her side, looming over her. "You didn't work last night, dammit. I was at the Toucan, and you weren't."

"You're lying. You never come by on Wednesdays. Never."

That she knew his schedule both surprised and pleased him. Still, Ry was so damned worked up, the only thing that would calm him down would be her concession to tell him the truth. "Do you have anything new to add to your story?" he pressed.

"Yes. If you insist on keeping me here against my will, I'm going to make your life a living hell."

He leaned forward, his face coming within inches of hers. "A weak threat, baby. I've already been to hell and back on account of you, so I'll be on familiar ground."

His words were as swift and solid as a hard slap. She drew back as if she'd physically felt it, then quickly looked away. "Get out of here."

Too late Ry realized the impact of his words. He'd made it sound as if he'd regretted the time they'd spent together. "Dammit, Margo! I never meant—"

"Get out of here," she demanded.

Dropping down on one knee beside the bed, he clasped her jaw and forced her to look at him. "That came out wrong. I didn't mean—"

"I said, get out!"

"We're both tired and worked up, saying things we don't mean," Ry insisted.

"I mean everything I say." She shoved his hand away. "I loathe the smell of you and the sound of your voice. I hate the way—"

"I taught you to kiss?"

His ego bruised, his frustration high, Ry leaned forward and took her mouth hard and fast. He knew it was wrong, knew the consequences of such a weakness. Only, she'd shattered his control and now it was too late to retreat.

He let her fight him until she was too weak to continue. Once she'd slumped against the headboard in defeat, he boldly took more, forcing his tongue between her lips to taste her for the first time in two long years.

It wasn't fair. Of all the cops in New Orleans, what were the odds that Ry would get assigned to the DuBay Pier murder?

Margo glanced at the clock on the nightstand. It was nearly noon, the day hot and slipping by miserably slowly. Absently she reached up and touched her bruised lips. She had never expected Ry to kiss her. But he was not a man to trifle with, and he'd proven that by punishing her swiftly for goading him.

And now what? The thought of spending more time with him after that kiss frightened her almost as much as not knowing where Blu was. She heard the radio station being switched on in the kitchen downstairs, and it reminded her that Ry had left his partner behind this morning to ensure she kept her promise to remain in his home. Jackson Ward had spent most of the day lounging in the hammock on the veranda. The tall, dark-haired man looked like a linebacker for the New Orleans Saints.

Her jailer may be big, Margo reasoned, but Brodie was his equal in size, and when he came for her, no one would stop her from leaving with him—not Ry or Jackson Ward.

Tired of watching the clock, Margo sank into the tufted chair to pout. She touched her lips again, remembered the moment she knew Ry was going to kiss her. Remembered the rush of heat, the violent shiver. Not wanting to analyze what had happened after that, she forced it all from her mind and concentrated on Blu. She had to believe he was alive. She also had to believe that whatever she'd witnessed last night wasn't in any way her brother's fault; Blu had just been in the wrong place at the wrong time, as she had been.

It was true Blu lived on the edge, but he didn't deal with men who used guns as easily as they used the bathroom. Well, he didn't normally hang out with cops, either, but then she was sure Blu would be able to explain why he'd been meeting one on a lonely pier at night.

Instead of her headache going away, the damn thing intensified. So much so, Margo was forced to go in search of some relief. What she found once she opened the medicine cabinet in the bathroom, however, had her dropping her jaw in shock—Ry owned a pharmaceutical so complete it could supply the entire neighborhood.

"He died instantly," the medical examiner told Ry. "AK-47, just like you figured."

Ry rubbed his jaw. "Time of death?"

"Eight o'clock, maybe a little earlier. He didn't feel a thing, honest, Ry. Pop, and he was sleeping."

"If you say so, Andy." Ry was exhausted, but he was determined to make some headway on the case before day's end. He picked up the report and scanned it, his instincts working overtime. He just couldn't get past the feeling that Margo had been on DuBay Pier last night. He wanted to be wrong, prayed for a witness to suddenly materialize and point him in a different direction, but he didn't think it was going to happen.

"You all right?" Andy asked. "Burelly wasn't a close friend of yours, was he?"

Ry glanced up at Andy Grecco. The medical examiner was in his early forties, wore his hair as cleanly cut as any military man, then threw the look all away by wearing a diamond in his ear and red tennis shoes. "No, Andy, we weren't close. What about the blood?"

"I'm still working on that. I'll give you a call."

Ry left the precinct digging for a cigarette. Lighting up, he barely acknowledged the heat by shoving his shirtsleeves up his muscled forearms and unbuttoning the top two buttons of his lightweight shirt. He climbed into the Blazer and swung into the busy traffic flow like a seasoned taxi driver, ignoring the car that honked in protest—he was late to meet Goddard at the Toucan.

Again, for the second time in less than an hour, Ry found himself thinking about Margo's warm lips. He'd had no business losing control like that. He should have kept his distance, knew about the hell he would unleash if he didn't. But regret it? How could he regret it when his reward had been feeling her shudder, then having her tilt her head back to allow him to taste her more completely. And now that moment was forever locked in his mind, eating at his libido like a desert parasite on holiday.

Ry parked his Blazer on the street, slipped through the courtyard and entered the back door of the Toucan. The lunch crowd was in full swing, the heady aroma of Thursday's special moving through the air as Tony's gumbo was leaving the kitchen by the gallons.

Since Ry was a regular, no one gave him a second look as he sauntered down the back hall to the restrooms. He found Goddard lounging against the wall next to the phone booth. He nodded, walked past and into the public facility. A few moments later Goddard joined him. They waited until the two men taking simultaneous leaks had pulled it together and left before Ry asked, "What do you got?"

"Word is somebody lost some mighty expensive merchandise."

"What kind of merchandise?"

"Don't know. The way I heard it, the goods were stolen a few days ago. Last night they were supposed to be recovered, only somethin' went wrong."

"I don't follow."

"You can't recover stolen goods off a dead man

unless he's got it on him. Whoever was on that pier last night was no doubt meetin' a buyer when the original owner got wind of it.''

"You saying Mickey was making a dirty deal on DuBay Pier last night?" That was hard for Ry to believe, but stranger things had happened.

"Ain't sayin' he was or wasn't. Could be he was set up or doin' someone a favor. You know it ain't always black-and-white, Superman. Could be a number of reasons why the suit went to sleep—anxious fingers, stupidity. Some guys just get off on killin' cops. Or maybe they didn't like the color of his suit." God chuckled at his own joke.

"Got a name for me?"

"Not yet." God scratched his chest. "But I ain't done askin' around."

"I want you to find Blu duFray." Ry handed Goddard a hundred-dollar bill. "That should keep you fed for a couple of days and buy transportation to speed things up."

"You mean take a cab?" Ry watched God's eyes go wide. "I got my reputation to consider, Superman. Takin' a cab is against principles."

"Take one, anyway. I'm in a hurry."

Goddard stashed the hundred in his threadbare pants pocket. "What you want duFray for? You don't think he shot the suit, do you? We both know Blu's too smart for that. If'n he wanted someone dead he'd just haul him out to the Gulf and sink him."

"Just find him," Ry said. "It's worth an extra fifty if you do."

Goddard walked to the urinal and unzipped his

pants. Over his shoulder he said, "I don't think Blu's your cop killer."

Ry had his hand on the door ready to leave. He turned back. "I never said he was. I just want to talk to him. Do I need to mention you should watch your back? Sloppy work don't pay dividends."

"I hear what you're sayin'." Goddard readjusted his pants, then headed for the sink to scrub his hands. "Don't get kilt. Don't plan on it, at least not before I have a bowl of that gumbo I smell."

"I'm sure Mickey didn't plan on it, either, when he stepped into his pants yesterday morning." That said, Ry strolled out the door and located the phone in the hall.

Three rings later Jackson drawled, "She's fine. Well, maybe not fine, but she's still here."

"Lucky for you." Ry filled his partner in on what he'd learned from God, then asked, "Has she used the phone?"

"Yeah. I left the portable on the table like you suggested. She took the bait."

"And?"

"She made two calls."

"Did you run back the tape?"

"Right away. There wasn't much on it. A few choice words of frustration is all. Guess whoever she tried to call wasn't home. I'll trace the numbers."

"I already got a pretty good idea who she called, but go ahead. If it isn't her brother's number, it'll be Brodie Hewitt's." Ry tried to hide the irritation in his voice. "I've got a lead to check out, then an errand to run. Should be back by six. Keep your eyes open. If she gets through to Hewitt and he shows up, book him for trespassing and handcuff him to something solid. He can be an ornery son of a bitch.''

Back in his Blazer, Ry headed west to Canal Street. From there he turned north to hook up with Loyola Avenue. He figured the key he'd found in Margo's jeans belonged to a storage locker of some kind. He would check the bus terminal first, then Amtrack. Parking, he entered the bus station only to find the numbers on the key were too high. Back in his car, fifteen minutes later, he hit the jackpot at the train depot. He slipped on a pair of rubber gloves he carried in his pocket, then promptly opened the locker.

Ry was used to dead ends but the empty locker soured his already-bad mood in a heartbeat. He had hoped for a solid piece of evidence. Something concrete that would point a finger far enough away from Margo to ease his mind and assure him it would be safe to send her back to her apartment. Only there was no black-and-white evidence; nothing but a crumpled-up piece of garbage on the bottom of the locker floor.

Ry returned to his office and spent the next hour combing Mickey's caseload in hopes of finding a name or a place where he could start his investigation. He went back six full months, only there was nothing unusual to attract his attention. Another hour passed while he made and returned several phone calls. On his way out, he'd been asked to stop by Chief Blais's office.

He rapped on Clide's door, stuck his head inside. ''You wanted to see me, Chief?''

''Come in for a minute, Ry.'' The chief stubbed out his fat cigar and leaned back in his chair.

Ry slipped through the door and closed it behind him. Taking a seat, he said, "If you want to know what I've got on the Burelly case, it's too early."

"There's nothing?" Clide stroked his silver mustache. "The boys upstairs want this wrapped up quickly. How about one of your hunches? Got a theory? You usually do, and it's usually dead right when the leg work's done."

Ry had already decided he wouldn't let go of anything he couldn't prove. And so far he had no proof Margo had been on the pier last night. Yes, he did have a hunch, but he didn't intend to offer it now. Once he had some concrete evidence, he would be forced to make a decision, but until then he would keep what he knew between himself and Jackson. "I've got some leads to check out, maybe after that."

Clide relaxed back in his chair and rested his hand on his thick belly. "I know you're working short-handed. I could assign someone to help out."

"I'm getting used to solo."

"You could put in for a new partner. I'd understand." He pointed to the bottle of antacid on his desk. "Jackson Ward's the main reason I got an ulcer, he'll likely give you one, too, if you don't walk away."

"He's a good cop, Clide."

"He's a pain in the ass," Clide insisted. "Now I know why the Chicago PD got rid of him."

Ry grinned. "I thought you said he came here voluntarily."

"It had to be a damn lie."

"Come on, Clide, Jackson's a smart cop and we need him."

"A smart aleck, you mean."

"From what I hear, he's just like you were when you were in the field."

"The hell you say! I never told the commissioner his dog could run this office better than he could. Believe me, I wanted to, at least twice a week, but that's not how it's done around here. You know that better than anyone, Ry. In this job you're expected to swallow a lot of bull and do it with a smile."

Ry couldn't argue with that. There were a dozen sides to law enforcement and half of them had nothing to do with the job specifically and everything to do with politics within the precinct. But the truth was, rather than work with someone he didn't know or trust, Ry would be content with Jackson even on a part-time basis. Ironically, on this particular case, Jackson's suspension was proving to be an asset.

It was after four by the time Ry left the precinct and parked in front of Margo's apartment building. As he assessed the drab exterior, he noted numerous repairs that were long overdue. But repairs were expensive and that expense had to be recovered somehow—usually with higher rent. In this neighborhood that would put most of the tenants out on the street.

When he'd first heard Margo had moved to the Cypress Apartments after their breakup, Ry swore he wouldn't allow her to live in such a dump. Then he'd thought better of his interference. After all, he had given up his right to meddle in her life, and as much as he'd hated keeping his mouth shut, he had. At least he had until last night.

Inside the building, Ry scaled the scarred wood staircase to the second story. He was about to pull a handy little device from his pocket to let himself into Margo's apartment when he noticed the door ajar. He went for his gun instead and eased the door open. What he found sickened him. Everything Margo owned had been destroyed.

Furious, Ry stepped inside and closed the door behind him. His gun remained in his hand, though he was sure the vandals were long gone. He stared at the mess; a busted rocker, the shredded couch, plants overturned and walked on. Step by step, room by room, he assessed the senseless destruction, barely able to contain his outrage. And through it all his hunch kept getting stronger.

He jammed his gun back into his holster and located Margo's phone in the kitchen. Surprised to find it in one piece, he hit rewind, then played back the messages. She'd had three calls: one from her mother asking her to call back, and the other two callers hadn't identified themselves. They had simply let the time run out in deliberate silence.

Chapter 5

By five in the afternoon, Margo had searched every inch of Ry's house. Concluding that he must have taken Blu's key with him, she gave up and went in search of her clothes. She was beginning to think Ry had taken them, too, when she found her jeans in the trash beneath the kitchen sink, along with her ruined shirt. Furious that he would deliberately toss her jeans, she swore him to hell, then moved to stand at the window overlooking the backyard.

Absently Margo stroked the yellow curtain at the kitchen window. As much as she hated to admit it, Ry's home was lovely. The kitchen was bright and warm, a bit too yellow, she thought, but it kept things cheery. Best of all was the backyard and the double swing that hung between a pair of giant oak trees. The shady trees were enormous, the branches sturdy for climbing. She'd always wanted to climb trees as a kid, but there hadn't been any in her neigh-

borhood, just row after row of shops and storefronts
squeezed into a compact line.

Mesmerized by the backyard, Margo pulled out a
chair and sat at the kitchen table. The well-placed
windows offered a grand view of a beautiful flower
garden, and before she knew it, she'd frittered an
hour away daydreaming about owning her own little
piece of heaven just like this, with room enough to
raise a half dozen kids.

When her stomach growled, Margo forced herself
up and crossed the pale-yellow tile floor to retrieve
a carton of eggs from a shelf in the refrigerator.
Hungry, glad for the distraction, she was about to
scramble some eggs when the back door opened and
in strolled Ry with a grocery bag under his arm. He
was wearing a lightweight blue shirt, glove-soft
worn jeans and boots.

He glanced at the eggs. "You're supposed to be
in bed resting. What the hell do you think you're
doing?"

"Whatever I feel like doing," Margo snapped
back. She saw his interest travel to her scant attire,
and it reminded her of where she'd found her jeans.
"How dare you toss my jeans in the garbage with
the coffee grounds. That's all I had to wear."

With no remorse in his tone or expression, he
said, "I wasn't so sure Jackson would be able to
handle you, so I took a precautionary measure." He
gave her slender legs another hard look. "It seemed
like a good idea at the time."

"I said I'd stay put. You didn't need to ruin my
jeans."

"You've skipped on me before, remember? I had

two cops on your tail, plus you'd promised to stay put that time, too.''

The incident he was referring to had taken place a few days before he'd left her. He'd become overly protective all of a sudden, demanding that she tell him where she was going every minute of the day. Then came a ridiculous curfew he'd expected her to abide by. The last straw had been the two plain-clothes cops he'd assigned to tail her as if she was a criminal.

She'd protested of course, and threatened, but he hadn't listened to one word. She'd had no choice but to ditch the tail and set Ry straight—she was not the kind of woman who would allow any man total control of her. She'd found him that night in the middle of a homicide on Bourbon Street. When she'd tapped him on the shoulder and he'd turned around, the black look he'd worn had been almost scary. Two days later he'd broken off with her.

''You should be lying down and taking it easy, don't you think?'' He moved further into the room and placed the bag on the table.

''I was.'' Margo told the lie with conviction. ''I just got up a little while ago.''

She had no intention of confessing she'd swiped the phone Jackson had left on the table and called for help, not that it had done her any good. She wouldn't tell him she'd searched every inch of his home looking for Blu's key, either—all eight closets, every drawer in every room, the kitchen pantry and the attic.

No, she hadn't found the key, but she had reacquainted herself with Ryland Archard. She'd learned his simple taste in clothes hadn't changed: he still wore jeans 90 percent of the time and lightweight cotton shirts and T-shirts. She'd found three identical pairs of brown cowboy boots in the closet, and one tan suit jacket. A subtle change was his preference in underwear. He now wore briefs, silk ones, and scraped his face with an electric razor instead of a straight edge. Then there were the true-crime novels. She had found them everywhere. There were as many books in his house as there were prescription drugs.

Margo felt his gaze on her bare legs again and stiffened. "What are you staring at? Legs are nothing new."

"True, everybody has a pair," he agreed. "But some are nicer to look at than others. You always did have great legs." He pulled a takeout container from the bag. "I suppose Tony's menu isn't all that special any longer. Still, the Toucan's shrimp is some of the best in the city."

"You stopped by the lounge? Why?"

He looked up. "To pick up the food."

"What else?"

He pulled a second container from the bag. "I was curious what sort of a mood Tony would be in after a secretary at the precinct gave him a call pretending to be a friend of yours. She told him you were going to be gone at least four days, possibly a week."

"Four days! A week! I can't afford to take that many days off." Margo called him a filthy name, then started for the door. By the time she rounded the table, Ry was blocking her escape. "Get out of my way."

"Aren't you forgetting something?" He gave her

a quick head-to-toe. "You can't leave the house dressed like that. Or rather, undressed, like that."

"Watch me." She darted past him and swung the door open. But before she took two steps onto the veranda, he grabbed her from behind and pulled her close, fusing her backside to his hard groin. Margo gasped with the knowledge of what she was up against and went still.

"That's right," he whispered in her ear, "I'm in the same condition I was last night. I've never lied about how much you turn me on, and that kiss this morning—"

"Was your idea," Margo hissed, "not mine." She kicked backward and clipped him hard in the shin.

"Ouch!" He tightened his hold on her. "Take it easy. You're going to rip open those stitches if you're not careful."

"I don't care." Margo kept fighting him. "All I want is to go home."

"That's not going to be possible now."

His words cut through her anger, and Margo stopped struggling. "What do you mean by that?"

Nudging her along, he half guided, half carried her back into the kitchen. After kicking the door shut, he let go of her.

Margo spun around quickly. "Answer me, dammit! What's happened?"

"I went to your apartment to pick up some clean clothes for you, and someone had gotten there first."

"Meaning?"

"Meaning everything you own was either smashed or shredded sometime last night or this morning. Your clothes…I'd say 10 percent made it. They're in the Blazer.''

"My plants?"

He shook his head.

"All of them?"

"I'm sorry, baby."

Stunned by what she was hearing, Margo turned away from him. "Why?" she muttered. "Why would they do that?"

"They?" He reached out and turned her to face him. "Tell me who *they* are."

"I don't know."

"Come on, Margo. I'm not stupid, and I resent like hell you thinking I am. I don't know what's going on, but it's damn obvious whoever shot you isn't through with you yet. Now that might not bother you, but it riles the hell out of me."

Margo frowned. "I don't see why it should."

"Plants and clothes are replaceable. But your life isn't, baby, that's why!"

When he mentioned the plants again, she felt physically sick. She knew it was crazy to feel so strongly over a bunch of plants, but the plants had been a part of her childhood dreams, the only part that she'd been able to realize. What Ry said about her clothes was true enough, they could be replaced. Her furniture had been secondhand. But the plants…

"Did you hear me, Margo? I want your cooperation, starting right now."

It wasn't fair, she decided. She'd agreed to take a handful of harmless pictures. A simple matter that required little or no skill and a small amount of time. Easy, right?

"It's time you trusted me. You came here last night. That must mean—"

"I told you, I didn't want to upset Mama."

"You can trust me, baby."

Margo wanted to trust someone, especially since Blu and Brodie had all but deserted her in her hour of need. But the truth was, she couldn't trust a man who had promised her the moon and the stars, then within a month's time had simply walked away. Chin raised, she slowly pulled herself together. "I'm tired. I'm going upstairs."

"Not before you eat something."

"I'm not hungry."

He flipped the top open on the takeout carton, releasing the aroma of grilled shrimp swimming in garlic butter. It was like a swift dose of déjà vu, and to Margo's horror her stomach promptly reacted with a sudden, fierce growl of satisfaction and betrayal.

Ry glanced her way, his intense expression of moments ago softening slightly. "I guess I chose right."

"I'm not sharing takeout with you," Margo insisted, recalling all the shared cartons of shrimp late at night in his apartment. They had lived for the nights. It had been a wicked, wild ride, the happiest time of her life.

He ignored her outburst and headed for the cupboard. Moments later the table was set with the shrimp and fettucini cartons placed in the middle.

"If you think feeding me old favorites is going to gain you some kind of edge, you can forget it. Recycling the past is a waste of energy."

"You're overreacting, Margo. The fettucini was today's special."

"Liar. On Thursdays it's gumbo with an andouille sandwich."

While she glared at him, he had the audacity to grin. "Okay, so I ordered off the menu." He went to the fridge, retrieved a yellow water pitcher and filled the yellow glasses, then set the pitcher on the table. "How's your arm?"

"Good as new."

"I doubt that. Any redness or swelling?"

Margo didn't answer. All day she'd noticed a tightness surrounding the stitches, but she wasn't about to mention it. She didn't want Ry playing doctor again. That would give him the opportunity to touch her, and she didn't think she could bear that. His kiss was still warm on her lips, a painful reminder that she needed to be on guard. He had manipulated her before; what were the odds that he could do it again?

"After supper I'll take a look."

"No, you won't. I said my arm's fine."

"A fresh bandage couldn't hurt." He pulled out a chair close to the window and gestured for her to take a seat. When Margo didn't budge, he said, "We both know you have a stubborn streak, but there's nothing to gain by not eating, Margo. Except maybe getting sick and missing more days at work."

Hating him for being right, Margo settled on the chair. Just as he was about to join her, he paused, reached into his shirt pocket and produced a bottle of pills. Setting them next to her water glass, he said, "I stopped by the drugstore and got you an antibiotic to fight infection."

Margo cradled her aching arm in her lap. "I already told you my arm's fine. Besides, I don't take pills, remember? But if I did, your medicine cabinet would be the first place I'd check. You must have something in there for every occasion."

He ignored the jibe and pointed to the bottle. "You'll take these. It's just a strong antibiotic to fight infection." When she didn't reach for the pills, he arched a brow, then leaned forward to look straight into her eyes. "I'm not going to fight you every step of the way here, Margo. If you don't want to be treated like a child, stop acting like one."

When she still didn't move, he sighed and scooped up a spoonful of fettucini and shrimp and plopped it on her plate. "A bite of food, then swallow two pills."

Furious with him, afraid to allow herself to give in an inch, she argued, "And if I don't?"

He offered her a tight smile. "You wouldn't want me to have to sit on you and force them down your throat, would you? That's what I used to do to the calves back home on the ranch. And for the record, I won every round and I wasn't half the size I am now." He relaxed his back against the chair and rested his elbow on the table. "Take the pills, Margo. You've got enough problems. You don't need to spike a fever in the middle of the night or have me wrestling you to the floor to prove I'm bigger than you."

Angry, Margo picked up her fork and poked a shrimp into her mouth, then snatched up the pills. She shook two into her hand and tossed them to the back of her throat. After emptying her water glass, she slammed it back on the table and attempted to stand.

Ry's hand reached out quickly and gripped her bare knee. "I also had to force feed some of those calves. Sometimes they were too stubborn to know what was good for them all the way around. You don't need me steering your fork, do you?"

Margo pinched the skin on the top of his hand hard enough to make him yelp, then let go. "You forgot napkins," she told him. "You can't eat Tony's shrimp without napkins. I was going to get some paper towels."

Margo glanced around until she spied the paper towels, *yellow paper towels.* Did he like the color yellow or what? Every room in his house had something yellow in it.

"I've got napkins," he offered. "I'll get them."

Margo watched as he went to one of the many drawers in the kitchen, withdrew a stack of *yellow*-and-white-striped napkins, and brought them back to the table. Once he was seated again, serving himself a healthy portion of shrimp and fettucini, she said, "Tell me about my apartment."

He looked up. "There's not much to tell. If they didn't break it they took it. All except a couple of pairs of ragged jeans and a few T-shirts." He stabbed a shrimp, then jammed it into his mouth and chewed. And all the time he was giving her a long, hard look. Finally, he asked, "Feel like telling me the truth yet? Why someone would want to shoot you, steal your underwear and destroy everything else?"

"My underwear?"

"Yeah. I didn't find any underwear among the

destroyed clothing. You still wear underwear, don't you?''

Incensed, Margo narrowed her eyes. "Of course I do."

"Who's after you, Margo?"

"I don't know."

"Did you see something you shouldn't have?"

"I don't know.

"How is Blu involved?"

"I don't..." Margo swore. "Blu's not involved. And that, Detective, is the truth. Whether you choose to believe it is up to you."

"The story last night was pure fiction, wasn't it. And you're still lying to me right now. Why?"

Stubbornly Margo remained silent.

Another minute passed before he said, "Jackson will be staying at your apartment tonight. If someone backtracks for any reason, we'll pick them up."

Surprised by the information, Margo's mood suddenly improved. If Ry was the only one watching her tonight it would make it easier to escape—he had to sleep sometime. "You said my clothes are in your Blazer?"

"I'll bring them in after supper." He drained his water glass. "When I was at your apartment I checked your answering machine. Your mother called."

"She called?"

"I want you to call her back. If she wants to see you, make up some reason why you can't. And make sure she knows you won't be at your apartment for a few days."

He was right about keeping her mother away from the apartment, Margo decided. She didn't want to escalate her mother's blood pressure or place her in danger. But how could she keep her away without lying to her? It didn't bother her to lie to Ry, and making up a story to Tony had been for a good reason—Blu had needed her help. She had never lied to her mother, she didn't even know if she could convincingly. Voicing her concern, she said, "I can't lie to Mama."

"But you can lie to me."

"Any day of the week."

He swore crudely.

Margo laid down her fork. "What? What is that look? Disappointment, shock?"

"Both. We never lied to each other."

Margo sniffed. "You mean I never lied because I was too stupid and gullible." The memories suddenly tasted bitter. "Don't bother trying to make me feel guilty, Ry. I owe you nothing."

She couldn't be sure, but he looked as if he flinched. "You're right. You don't owe me anything, but your mother deserves to be safe, so call her and tell her you're staying with a friend for a few days. Call her, or I will."

She hated him for being right, but she would call her mother. And if she had to lie, it would be just this once.

"Has your place been broken into before?"

Margo picked up her fork and played with her fettucini. "Yes. So it could have been just—"

"A random burglary? We both know these creeps didn't break in to lift your radio. They were sent to deliver a strong message and it was damn clear. You've pissed someone off, and not just a little bit. What if you had been home when they broke in?

Have you thought about what would have happened?''

Of course she had thought about that. But what was she going to do? She didn't know who was after her, not a clue.

"You just don't get it, do you? The place was gutted, dammit! Smashed to hell!''

Margo winced at the force of his words. "My stuff was old. It wasn't worth much.''

"And you! What is your life worth?'' He tossed the fork at his plate and abruptly stood. "Why do you do that?''

"Do what?''

"Cheapen yourself like that. You've done it before, and I don't like it. You talk like you're second in importance to everyone else. To Blu, to your mother. You deserve first class if that's what you want. Whatever the hell it is you want, dammit!''

Amused that he was shouting again, Margo said, "I'll remember that next time I want a new car. I'll tell the salesman he can bill you.''

"This isn't a joke, Margo.''

"I'm just saying the furnishings didn't have any great value. The plants didn't, either, but they were living things. Innocent and harmless.''

"I'll replace the plants.''

"I don't want you replacing the plants or anything else.''

"Just a minute ago you were willing to let me buy you a new car.''

"You know I wouldn't take a dime from you,'' Margo scoffed.

He stared her down. Finally he said, "When your apartment was broken into before, what was taken?''

"Some money. CD's My...*radio*."

"Did you report it?"

"No."

He sat back down. "Why not?"

"I know the drill, Detective Archard. No prints, no suspects. Or, if the department was lucky enough to pull a print, the print would need to be on file to do any good."

He frowned. "You make us sound useless."

"You said that, I didn't."

"But you think it." A mix of emotions changed the color of his eyes to a dark-navy.

"I understand your sensitivity on the subject. It comes from needing to validate the past ten years, and the best way to do that is to believe in the system. If you didn't, it would seem pretty silly playing cops and robbers at your age, right?"

His frown pinched his brows together. "This job is for real, Margo. I resent like hell you implying otherwise. I believe in what I do, and I've paid a fat price for being good at it. If you don't respect me as a man, at least respect me for what I do."

He looked stricken—completely insulted, but Margo refused to apologize. "It's not just about me catching the bad guys and getting them off the streets. It's about drug dealers getting fat off restless, mixed-up kids, it's about husbands thinking they have a right to beat their wives. It's about making a difference daily wherever you can. It's about giving a damn."

"Saint Ryland Archard to the rescue." Margo sniffed, then shook her head. "I hate to tell you this, Ry, but in my book you're no saint. What you give a damn about is anyone's guess. Two years ago it certainly wasn't about a young woman who idolized the ground you walked on. A woman you promised to love forever.''

"Margo—"

"No! Don't preach to me about your almighty goodness, Detective Archard, because I've had an altogether different experience where you're concerned. And speaking about paid prices. I did my time on the bottom, thanks to you.''

Margo hadn't meant to confess anything personal, but it was too late. She'd implied Ry hadn't just hurt her, but that the hurt had been devastating. Feeling the need to hurt him in order to recover a little dignity, she continued. "They say you learn the most from rejection and disappointment. If that's true, I suppose I should thank you. I don't trust easily, and I don't wear my heart on my sleeve anymore. Best of all, I don't need a man in my life to be happy. Family is most important.''

"You're talking about Blu.''

"Yes. He's not only the best brother in the world, but my best friend.''

"Saint Blu duFray to the rescue," he mocked, as she had mocked him. "If that's the case, and he's so wonderful, why aren't you with him right now? Why come to me?'' Before Margo could speak, he said, "I'll tell you why. Because he's the reason you're in this mess. Mr. Wonderful is the reason you've got a bullet hole in your arm and an apartment that looks like it was taken apart by gremlins. I told you two years ago that if you needed anything I would—''

"Would what? Take Blu's place and play big brother one weekend a month, or whenever you got bored? Or did you have something else in mind? Were you planning on taking me to bed for a pity—''

''Stop it!''

''You can't be everyone's saint, Ry. Some of us have to save ourselves or choke on our own poison. You were my poison—I admit that. But like other addictions, recovery is a simple process once you learn the rules.''

''And you learned the rules? You're smart?''

''Smart enough to stay away from you.'' Again feeling vulnerable, Margo rescued her pride in the only way she could. ''I really should thank you— the entire experience was quite an education. Best of all was the sex education. A straight-A student, you once said. Brodie agrees and compliments me often.''

The look of hurt in his eyes should have made Margo feel ashamed, but she refused to let it. After all, he was the one who had rejected her. The one who had walked away and never looked back.

The sudden ring of the telephone made Margo jump. Settling back in her chair, she waited for Ry to answer it, hoping all the while that it was Blu or Brodie.

He reached for the phone where it hung on the wall above the kitchen table. ''Archard, here.''

Margo watched Ry's scowl disappear.

''Tonight? No, I won't be there.'' He offered a false laugh as he cradled the phone next to his ear. ''No, I can't.'' His gaze locked on Margo. ''No really, I can't. Why? That's right, I'm working on a case. Yes, this very minute.''

Margo sensed the caller was a woman, a persistent woman who obviously wasn't used to taking no for an answer.

"Time off? What's that?" Another put-on laugh. "It goes with the job, I guess. Most days I'm about as reliable as—"

"Cheap rubber soles." Margo's voice was clear as a bell.

Ry mouthed for her to keep quiet, which she responded to with a cheesy grin, then her tongue. Moments later he hung up the phone.

"Don't let me ruin your evening." Margo pushed her half-eaten supper aside and stood. "I'll just—"

"Take off the minute I walk out the door. Don't kid yourself, baby. I know exactly what's running through that head of yours."

Margo hoped not. She should be formulating an escape plan, or racking her brain trying to think of a way to help Blu. Certainly, she should be coming up with a fail-safe lie to tell her mother about why she wouldn't be at her apartment for the next few days. But instead all she could think about was that phone call and who the woman was on the other end.

She shouldn't care, not one damn bit. Then why did she?

Chapter 6

"Hi, Mama, it's me." Margo stood at the window with the phone cupped to her ear while Ry cleaned the supper dishes off the table. "I got your message. Is everything all right? Yes, I know I always call you before nine every morning."

Margo turned to catch Ry watching her, and she lowered her voice. "What? I'm sorry, Mama. Angie—you remember Angie, don't you? I introduced her to you at the Toucan months ago. Yes, she's the pretty blond waitress with the twins. That's right, the one who's husband left her. Well, she's sick, so I volunteered to help her out with the kids. That's why my morning routine got thrown off. Yes, Mama, kids are a lot of work. What was that? No, it doesn't look like her husband is coming back. Yes, I know, Mama, the men in this city are all tomcats. Except for Papa, that's right. And Blu. Yes, you raised him to respect women. Brodie? Yes, Mama, he respects me.''

Margo heard Ry swear, then slam a cupboard door harder than necessary.

"The noise? Of course I heard it, Mama." Margo gave Ry an angry glare. "It's the twins. You know how kids are, they're as bad as grown men sometimes, acting up when someone's on the phone."

Another cupboard door slammed.

"A good swat on the behind? Yes, I intend to the minute I get off the phone. What was that? Blu didn't call you today, either. Don't worry, I'm sure he's…he's fine." Margo squeezed her eyes shut. She hated lying, hated having to pretend everything was fine when it wasn't fine at all. "If I see him I'll give him a piece of my mind for worrying you, okay? Good night, Mama. I love you, too."

When she hung up the phone and opened her eyes, Ry was standing over her right shoulder, so close she could feel his breath on her ear. Margo stiffened. "Learn anything interesting?"

"Actually, I did." He placed his hand on her shoulder and forced her to face him. "You don't know where he is, do you?"

"He?"

"Blu."

"No," Margo admitted easily. "But that's nothing new. Blu's as busy as I am."

"That's not what I meant and you know it. I can see it in your eyes, hear it in your voice. You're worried sick about him. He's in some kind of trouble, and he's dragged you into the middle of it, hasn't he?"

Margo tried to brush past him, but he reached out

and grabbed her wrist and reeled her in close. "I can help you. Let me."

"Let go!" Margo jerked her arm free and headed out of the kitchen and up the stairs. She heard him behind her. When she reached the bathroom, she whirled around and faced him. "I'm taking a bath. Go away."

"Give me a chance, Margo. I won't let you down this time."

"It's too late."

"I don't believe that."

"I don't care what you believe."

"You used to."

"I used to share my bath with a rubber duck, too. That doesn't mean I still do." That said, Margo stepped inside the bathroom, closed the door and locked it.

She was lying on his bed, swallowed up in his navy blue robe. She looked beautiful, sexy as hell, and in no better mood than when she'd slammed the bathroom door in his face.

"I told you I don't want you gawking at me or my arm. It's fine."

Ry ignored her protest and eased the robe off her shoulder. He noticed the redness around the stitches immediately. "Your arm isn't fine, dammit! It's infected. Swollen, too." Suddenly his own anger, the anger he'd been wrestling with for the past hour, was redirected at himself. "I should have taken you to the hospital last night. I never should have let you talk me into sewing you up. Come on, get up and I'll help you dress. We're going to the emergency room."

"I'm not going anywhere. Especially to the emergency room," she argued.

"Listen, Margo—"

"No, you listen. We'll hot pack it. That's what Mama would do."

Ry eased down next to her on the bed. "Infection can be very serious business, baby. Are you sure a hot pack will fix it? Maybe I didn't clean it well enough, or maybe I should have—"

"Oh, stop it. I won't sue you if my arm drops off. And besides, I'm taking the antibiotic, remember?"

Instead of easing his mind, her joke infuriated him. Ry stood quickly. "Get up. I'm taking you to the hospital."

"What? What did I say?"

"I resent like hell you making jokes about something this damn serious."

"You're overreacting. With all the gloom and doom you deal with every day I'd think this would just be routine for you. I always said you could use an overhaul on your sense of humor," she chastised. "You'd think it was your arm in danger of getting chopped off."

"No one's going to chop off your arm!"

"Okay, no more bad jokes. But it's my arm, so we'll do it my way and hot pack it." When Ry attempted to argue, she held up her hand. "Quit! You're going to sprout gray hair if you don't lighten up."

In the end Ry hot packed her arm the way she suggested, then bandaged it carefully. When he was finished, he said, "I got your clothes out of the

Blazer and hung them in the closet. I cleaned out a couple of drawers in my dresser for the T-shirts.''

"I don't want to stay in this room with you."

Ry strolled to the dresser. "You don't have a choice. This room has the only bed in the house." He pulled a peach-colored T-shirt from one of the drawers, draped it over his arm and came back to the bed. "Lets get you out of my robe and into something you can sleep in."

"Let's not."

Ry watched her pull his robe closer. "Are you cold?"

"No, just capable of dressing myself, thank you. Besides, you ogle me every chance you get."

"I don't ogle. I appreciate."

"Drooling like a dog isn't appreciation, it's disgusting."

"So I enjoy the sight of a naked woman in my bed. Most men do."

"Get out," she said, flaring up.

"You're kidding, right? I've seen all of you dozens of times. I know every inch of your body. Last night, I—"

"Last night I would have let Jack the Ripper take my clothes off. Leave or turn around."

"This is crazy, Margo." When she just sat there clutching the robe tighter, Ry sighed, laid the T-shirt next to her, then turned his back and crossed his arms over his chest. "We used to take showers together," he reminded. "Hell, we used to eat breakfast naked in bed."

"*Used to* are the important words. It means *not any longer*."

He heard her climb out of bed, heard his robe

drop to the floor. He turned to make sure she was all right—okay, so he knew she was all right. He caught a glimpse of her nakedness as the T-shirt drifted over her thighs and his guts tightened. She was so damn beautiful, and he was such a fool; a fool to think he could be this close to her and keep his hands off her. She'd called him her addiction. Well, the shrink he'd seen for six months had called Margo his. And the shrink had been right, at least about that much.

She glared at him when she realized he had turned around too soon. "I hope you don't plan on sleeping in that chair again tonight."

"Is that an invitation to share the bed?"

"In your dreams."

Every night, Ry wanted to say.

With a sniff she pulled back the comforter and climbed into the center of the bed, giving him a quick glimpse of her sweet backside covered in white satin. When she was comfortable, she glanced at him and said, "Haven't you left yet? Your partner kept watch from the veranda. It's just an idea, but it sounds good to me."

Ry unbuttoned his shirt and tossed it on the chair. "You want me to sleep outside?"

"This is New Orleans, not the North Pole. If that doesn't suit, you have four other bedrooms to pick from."

"Four empty bedrooms," Ry reminded.

She rested her back against the headboard. "Look at it as a way for you and one of the floors across the hall to get more intimately acquainted. Which hardwood floor sparks your fancy, Detective Archard?"

God, she was stunning to look at, Ry thought, letting her taunt go by unanswered.

"Isn't it considered a little odd to have bedrooms with no beds in them? What do your houseguests say? Or do they stay in this room with you when they visit?"

By the look on her face, she had surprised herself with the question. Ry watched as she took a sudden interest in the bed covering, her hand reaching out to smooth its surface. He considered lying, was tempted to offer a tall tale about the dozens of women he'd had as houseguests. So many, in fact, he couldn't remember their names.

The truth came easier. "Outside of Jackson hanging around a few evenings a week, you're the first houseguest I've had since I moved in here."

"Not even one blonde?"

There had been one blonde, but she hadn't stayed that long. "No, no blonde overnight." Again he watched her hand absently stroke the comforter. "If you need anything—"

Her hand stilled as if she'd just realized what she was doing. She met his gaze. "At the moment, just you sleeping somewhere else."

The moonlight highlighted her sleekness, outlined her shapely curves. Yes, Taber had to admit the Blu Devil's cruiser was worth taking a moment to admire. It wasn't new by any means, but the *Nightwing* had been kept in immaculate condition. At least forty-five feet long, she was equipped with a full-length spray rail and a roomy cabin below deck. It was small by Taber's standards, but her power-reaching lines and the craftsmanship were well defined.

No, Antos hadn't exaggerated—the cruiser was a rare beauty—but the *Nightwing* wasn't what Taber had on his mind as he signaled his driver to pull off the road. They still hadn't found Blu duFray or the missing merchandise, and though his men were working around the clock to produce both, they had come up short.

There were hundreds of rat holes in the city to disappear into, and from what Taber had recently learned about duFray, the man likely knew where all of them were. Still, it paid to be a demanding boss—his men knew what it would cost them if they didn't find duFray, and find him soon.

At least luck had been with him where the woman was concerned. Antos had brought him the information he'd anxiously been waiting for early that morning. It was the reason he'd been lured out to endure the sticky heat. He seldom went out; everything he wanted could be delivered to him. Even women could be obtained by a single snap of his fingers.

Only, the woman he wanted right now was being as elusive as her brother. Yes, the mystery woman on the pier was none other than Blu duFray's sister. More surprising—she was someone Taber knew. Not well, but he had enjoyed listening to her sing at the Toucan Lounge. He'd even gone so far as to name the little songbird ''Beautiful'' weeks ago.

Taber reached for the ice-blue chemise that lay in the seat beside him—one of the mementos Antos had brought to him from *her* dingy apartment. He lifted the satin to his nose and inhaled deeply. The erotic scent aroused him like nothing had in a long while and his newfound obsession gripped him harder.

So where was she hiding? Taber mused, refusing to believe the talented little singer was at the bottom of the river, that her valiant efforts had ended so tragically. He'd instructed Antos to check the hospitals and safe houses, but no one fitting her description had been admitted last night or this morning.

"There's movement on-board, sir," Antos informed.

Taber's gaze drifted to the cruiser riding the calm tide and the man who had suddenly appeared topside in the moonlight. The man was six-foot tall and thickly muscled. He stood looking off toward New Orleans, his shaggy brown hair tied back, his hands braced on the railing.

Brodie Hewitt was the foreman for Blu duFray's fishing fleet. Taber recognized him from the Toucan. Hewitt was also a close friend of the woman's. Did he know where she was hiding? Did he know if she'd survived the river?

The questions prompted an idea so rich and ingenious, Taber laughed out loud. Pleased with himself, he stuffed the blue silk into his pocket and got out of his car, ordering Antos to follow.

It was after midnight when Margo slipped from the bed and into a pair of jeans. As luck would have it, Ry had decided to sleep elsewhere. The noise across the hall an hour ago suggested he'd bedded down on a floor in one of his empty rooms.

Smiling, feeling confident about her planned escape, Margo crept into the hall and slowly descended the stairs. She let out her held breath as she reached the last step and walked past the living room entrance. The house was dark, but a small amount of moonlight shining through the windows fed her confidence, and she reached the kitchen without mishap. A few short steps brought her to the back door.

The night was sultry, the smell of jasmine heady as Margo slipped out the door onto the veranda. The quiet backyard gave her pause, and she hesitated to appreciate the solitude. Ry's home was like a secret hideaway, the tranquil eye in a turbulent storm. It was crazy, but Margo felt safe here. She had from the moment she'd slipped through the hedges last night. The two huge oaks that boarded one edge of the backyard reminded her of giant sentinels, their spidery limbs dressed in feathery Spanish moss. And ironically, the white ornate iron swing between the trees resembled the one in her childhood dreams.

It was everything she had ever wanted as a little girl—a home hidden away from the people who frequented the fish market. A house large enough to afford her children rooms of their own, with space enough in the backyard for them to climb trees, or simply breathe fresh air without being watched.

As a child Margo's family of four had lived on top of each other in a tiny three-room apartment above the fish market—the market crammed between two larger buildings on either side. The upstairs bedroom she'd shared with Blu had one window and it had overlooked an alley.

Oh, her family had loved each other fiercely, and that had been the most important thing. But a private place of her own had always been Margo's secret passion.

She inhaled deeply, then walked to the iron railing that wrapped the house with nostalgic charm. She should hurry and leave, but for just a moment she would imagine herself in the swing, and that this home was—

"Running off without saying goodbye?"

Margo gasped then whirled around. Ry lay sprawled in the large hammock only a few feet away. "I didn't see you," she blurted.

"No, I guess not."

He swung his legs over the side of the hammock and slowly stood. His bare chest gleamed in the moonlight, his long legs still encased in soft, worn jeans. They rode low on his narrow hips. His feet were bare, and there was an empty whiskey bottle beneath the hammock.

"I thought you were sleeping upstairs." Margo tried to ignore how good he looked in the moonlight.

"That's what I was hoping you'd think."

"So you pretended to go to sleep across the hall, when all the time you intended to sleep out here?"

"The best place to catch a thief, or a sneak in the middle of the night, is next to the door."

"I'm no thief and no sneak, either," Margo argued. "I couldn't sleep. I thought—"

"No more games, baby. We both know what you were about to do. Where were you going, back to your apartment or to the *Nightwing?*"

Margo didn't like the way he was looking at her. It wasn't the way a man looked at a woman he no longer cared about.

"Apartment or the *Nightwing?*" he asked again.

"The *Nightwing*," Margo admitted.

"To Blu?"

Margo swore. "Stop looking at me like that."

"If you don't like how I'm looking at you, you should have stayed in my bedroom with the door closed." His gaze slid over her breasts. "I remember this T-shirt, but not it being that tight."

Margo attempted to move past him and escape back inside, but he stepped sideways and blocked the door. She could smell the whiskey on his breath. He had never been much of a drinker in the old days. In the past year she'd seen him with a beer now and then at the Toucan, but rarely anything stronger. "Are you drunk?"

"I don't think so." He grinned. "I still know my name...yours, too." His expression sobered. "When you call Hewitt, does he normally pick up? Should he have today when you called?"

The question shocked her. "You tapped your own phone. That was a setup, too."

He stepped closer, allowing the moonlight to dance dreamily over his bare chest. Margo didn't want to notice, didn't want to admit that her heart-rate had doubled. She wanted the sight of him to disgust her, wanted back inside so she could start thinking of another way to escape before morning.

He reached up and ran his thumb over her marred cheek. It had turned a dark shade of blue. "Does it hurt?"

"Only when you touch it. So don't."

He dropped his hand. "How about your knees?"

"Let me go back inside, Ry."

"Do you think hot packing your arm will work?"

"I'll let you know in the morning. Let me go back inside, Ry."

He slowly brushed her hair off her shoulder. "Do you ever think about the way it was? How hot we burned?"

"I want to go back upstairs. Please, let me go."

He kept his hand in her hair, moving the strands around with his fingers. "I remember," he confessed. "All of it. Those helpless little noises you always made. The way you would hold your breath when I—"

"Stop it. You said no more games. Well this game is one I refuse to play with you."

"Does Hewitt make you burn? Burn the way I used to? Do you moan and fight it at first? Does he make your skin hot and your nipples turn to stone? Does he—"

"Yes. Yes to all of it." Margo needed a safety net for her emotions, needed to believe in what she was saying. If she didn't... He was looking at her as if something was going to happen between them, something profound and earth-shattering. Something that would make them both "burn." She'd already convinced herself that nothing like that could ever happen between them ever again.

He took a step closer, forcing her back against the railing. His hands gripped the cool iron on either side of her, surrounding her with his heat, his masculine scent. "I think you're lying about Hewitt. If you were getting what you need, you wouldn't have so much trouble keeping your body reined in right now."

Slowly he leaned into her, and a surge of blood rushed through Margo's veins. She swallowed hard and did her best to keep her chin up. "My body doesn't remember you. I don't feel anything for you."

He shook his head. "People are my business. I watch them, gauge their actions, their reactions. I listen for alterations in their breathing, watch their eyes. It's what I do, baby, and I do it better than most."

What he said was true; he did have a talent for reading people, that's what made him such a good cop. But she couldn't let him read her thoughts right now, she couldn't.

"Should we test my theory?"

"I hate you," Margo insisted.

"With good reason. But maybe not as much as you want to. I'm not reading *hate* right now."

Margo struggled to breathe, forced herself to look at him once more. "You always did have a healthy ego, Ry. But you're wrong. Right now you're making me—"

"Hotter than you've been in a long while."

"No. What you make me is sick."

It was the wrong thing to say. Instead of forcing him to back off, her words had tossed him a challenge. He reached up to trace her lower lip with the side of his thumb. Slowly, deliberately, he trailed a finger over her chin and down her neck.

Margo stood perfectly still. She cursed the fact that she hadn't taken the time to change her T-shirt. Her sensitive nipples had puckered against the worn-out cotton, and she knew Ry felt them against his hard chest.

"You're fighting for air," he whispered. "Your eyes are wider, and your body... Your body's caught and your brain knows it. Relax, Margo. Take a deep breath, then let it out slowly.''

As if she had no will of her own, she did as he told her. She drew in a solid breath then exhaled.

"Again."

"Please, Ry. Back off."

"It won't help, baby. There's only one thing that will help. It's got to get worse before it can get better." He gave her an inch, but it didn't last long. Suddenly his hand was between them, brushing his fingertips across her aching swollen breasts.

Margo jerked her gaze back to his. "Ry, stop! Stop right now. I want to go back inside. My arm hurts. The infection is—"

He shook his head, smiled a little sadly.

"I hate you!" she flared again.

"Like I said, you should. But even if you do, the one thing you can't deny is how much you want that memory we share."

"I can't want someone I hate."

His hand stilled. "I'm convinced a body has a homing instinct. It knows where it's the safest. Where it belongs, and to whom."

"My body doesn't belong to you," Margo argued. It couldn't, she thought with a sense of panic. If that was true, she'd be miserable her entire life.

There was no reason to stand there and listen to him any longer. No reason to carry this conversation further. Only, she was doing just that, standing frozen in place like a stone statue.

"Ry, please."

"Please, what?"

"What is it you want? Information? I don't have any to give you. Honest."

"Any good cop worth his salt is always ready to work out a deal for the sake of his case. I have to confess right now the case is the farthest thing from my mind." He smiled and it softened the intensity in his very blue eyes. "No, baby, what I want tonight is simple and selfish. I want to see you naked, fighting me a little and panting my name at the same time." His hands were suddenly on her, pulling her away from the railing and against his swollen arousal. "Here. Upstairs. In the grass. Where doesn't matter. But it's your call."

He was confusing her, purposely making her remember a time when all she had ever wanted was to be swallowed up in his arms, his powerful body setting her on fire. The memories were too profound to ever forget, but she had to forget the passion to save herself. She had to remember only the pain to keep from making a fool out of herself one more time.

Desperate to get away, to think clearly, she said, "You're right, Ry. It's my call, and I want you to let go. I don't want this."

This time when she tried to move, he dropped his hand and took a step back. Relieved, Margo hurried toward the door.

"Margo?"

She didn't turn around, but she hesitated in the doorway.

"Lock the bedroom door."

Chapter 7

Ry picked the lock in record time, then eased the bedroom door open. She was sitting in the middle of his bed, moonlight capturing her in a stream of light.

"I wasn't sure you'd remember," he drawled. "It's been a while since we've played this game."

"I remember the rules. Locked, you're welcome—unlocked, stay out."

It was a crazy game, one they had made up to sharpen his lock-picking skills. He'd told Margo if she was waiting for him in bed, it would give him more incentive.

"Are you sure this is what you want?" Ry asked, suddenly afraid that he'd pushed too hard downstairs on the veranda.

"Good sex is hard to turn down. The best is when there's no strings."

It wasn't exactly what Ry wanted to hear or agree

to, but tonight he would settle for a slice of the heaven he remembered. He would enjoy holding Margo close and be swept away by the feel of her sweet body against his. He would immerse himself in her heat and feast on that incredible rush of excitement that only came when she was the woman in his arms. Tonight he would be just a man hungry for the woman he loved.

She turned back the coverlet in invitation and revealed she was naked. "'In your arms, panting your name' will come as soon as you decide to join me, Ry. But it won't happen with you standing way over there."

He realized he'd frozen up. Ry supposed it was natural. He'd dreamed of this moment for two years, and now that it was here he was overwhelmed by the sight of her in his bed inviting him calmly and confidently to join her.

He strolled forward, stopping when his leg brushed the side of the bed. Her gaze shifted to his jeans, his arousal crammed painfully tight against his fly. Leaning forward, she boldly brushed her fingers over him. "Can I see, or have you turned shy in your old age?"

She had always felt the need to tease him. And it usually centered around their age difference. He'd reasoned that she'd always been a bit insecure when it came to the twelve years of experience he had on her. He'd never made an issue out of her inexperience when he'd taken her virginity, but he had always suspected it had worried her—she had so much pride.

Was that why she was trying so hard right now to be the aggressor? Or was it simply that Brodie had taken up where he'd left off two years ago, and Margo was just doing what came naturally?

Her fingers climbed his fly and rested an inch from the snap. When he didn't move, she hesitated and glanced up at him. "Am I going too fast for you?"

"What do you think?"

She licked her lips, then eyed his zipper. "I think I'm going to have a peek." She deftly unsnapped his jeans then slowly slid his zipper down. When she realized he had foregone underwear after his shower, she dropped her hands. As the seconds ticked by Ry's flesh began to tease the opening wider.

"What are you thinking, baby?"

"I'm thinking I'm impressed, Detective Archard." Her gaze found his. "For an old man, everything appears to be in working order."

She drew up on her knees, her hands skimming over his arousal, once, twice. She kept her eyes locked with his as her hot little fingers tortured him mercilessly over and over again. Ry finally closed his eyes, gave way to the moment. "Margo…" Her name came out in a tortured rush.

"Shhh. Everything seems to be nice and…hard. But then I haven't seen everything. Maybe your butt has turned saggy."

Ry opened his eyes and found her smiling. "You're teasing the wrong guy, baby."

"Are you going to pull your handcuffs out again and chain me to the bedpost?"

"Would you like it that way?" Ry had been waiting to touch her, holding off until he was sure she was fully committed to spending the night with him.

But he couldn't hold back any longer. He raised his hands and, starting at the backs of her legs, guided his fingers upward. When he reached the indent that gave shape to her wonderful backside, his fingers curved into her and parted her backside just a little. She sucked in a quick breath, gasped when he squeezed slightly, his fingers finding her warmth.

"Look at me." When she did as he asked, he said, "This kiss, the one coming up. Show me you remember what it was like for us. Kiss me crazy, baby."

When their lips met, she opened her mouth and eagerly accepted his tongue. Ry took full advantage, and a moment later he nearly swallowed her whole. And then he heard it, a little strangled noise at the back of her throat. The one she had always offered him when she was surrendering completely to him.

It had all been worth it, he decided, the guilt, the lonely nights. She was here in his arms. *Alive.* And, yes, kissing him crazy.

Without a doubt, Ry knew he would never again question the choice he'd made two years ago. As difficult as it had been, it was the only choice he could have made. He sighed, kissing her again, then once more.

His hands moved up her back to roam her lovely curves. He teased her delicate spine, then fondled her backside. Bringing her more solidly against his stony arousal. He murmured, "I'm burning."

"Me, too," she sighed.

"Need to be careful for your arm," he warned.

"My arm's fine," she whispered, "but the rest of me…"

Her words trailed off as she lowered her head to

nip at his bare chest. Ry moaned as her tongue
teased his right nipple, then went on to the left.
"These jeans look great on you, but it's time to
prove you're not all talk, old man." She sank lower
and kissed his stomach. Inching lower, her tongue
made a quick pass around his navel.

Ry felt her hands sink into his back pockets, felt
her slender fingers push his jeans off his hips.

"It's just sex," she murmured once more. "Say
it."

Her hot breath swept over him, her lips barely
grazing the tip of his stony hardness. She was teasing him so fiercely that Ry was ready to explode.
He reached out and pulled her back into his arms.
"Just sex," he agreed, then lifted her slightly to settle his hot mouth on one of her proud breasts.

She clung to him as he suckled first one mound
then the other.

"I need to be inside you," Ry murmured sliding
her back down his aroused body to kiss her hot little
mouth once more.

"I need you inside me," she agreed, pushing
away from him to lie down on the bed. Her long
legs stretched out to expose the nest of dark curls at
the junction of her thighs. She relaxed one leg,
opened a little.

Ry stepped out of his jeans and slid onto the bed.
She spread her thighs in welcome and he settled
between her long legs. "You're beautiful," he murmured, then kissed her and sent himself swiftly inside her.

It was like coming home, Ry thought as a flood
of heat jerked him hard, then closed tightly around
him. The sensation was so all-consuming, so emo-

tional, that he went still. He told himself to breathe,
to relax, but instead he started to shake.

''Ry...''

''Right here,'' he promised, hardly recognizing
his own voice. He was going to make a fool out of
himself, he thought.

He forced himself up on his elbows to gaze down
at her. He would have said something, but he
couldn't think of anything but three little words.
And *I love you* were the wrong words to say when
they had just agreed that this was only going to be
hot sex.

He had no intention of driving her away, not now.
Not when she was in his arms, feeding his dreams
and making them a reality.

Ry moved his hips, then, never losing sight of her
beautiful face, he drew back and sank deeper. She
arched up and bucked her hips against him. His
name on her lips and her frenzied little moans sent
a shudder ripping through him. And then, in one
powerful surge of hungry heat, the love storm began.

Forever and a lifetime, Ry vowed, that's how long
he would love her. He simply had no choice.

The addiction was back, and like any good addiction, it had left Margo hungry for more.

She stood at the bedroom window and gazed out
over the sun-filled backyard. She couldn't get last
night out of her mind. She was still reliving every
sweet, wild, insane moment. And she was wrestling
with the right and wrong of what she'd done, as
well.

She was consoling her conscience one minute,

then chastising herself the next. Mostly, though, she was glorying in the decadence of sated bliss.

When Ry had insisted she lock the bedroom door, she had realized he wasn't only giving her time to rethink his offer, but a way to act on her need without humiliating herself. After that it had been an easy decision to make—she'd locked the door, stripped off her clothes and gotten into his bed to wait.

Margo glanced back at the empty bed. An hour ago she had opened her eyes and she had known that she was alone in the big bed. She should have been thankful that Ry had given her time to pull herself together, but for pride's sake she had wanted to be the one to leave the bed first. Or maybe it had been for more selfish reasons, she decided—maybe if she had opened her eyes first she could have lingered to enjoy the sight of Ry's beautiful body lying next to her.

Yes, the addiction was back. In one weak moment she'd locked the door and thrown caution out the window. She could blame it on last night's sultry heat or the open-faced moon. Or she could blame it on Ry's handsome face and his hard, bare chest. Better still, on his powerful words of seduction.

But she wasn't going to. She would accept what had happened and view it as a man would—in the midst of chaos, she'd taken time out to refuel her body. Men had wild nights of consensual sex all the time, so why not a woman?

Margo's gaze caught sight of Jackson as he went to retrieve something from his late-model Ford pickup. Stepping away from the window, she decided a shower and clothes were in order. Then food; her stomach had already growled twice.

A half hour later Margo walked into the kitchen wearing last night's jeans and a lightweight white cotton shirt. As she headed for the fridge, the kitchen table caught her eye, and she stopped dead in her tracks—in the center sat a vase full of yellow roses.

Margo's heart began to pound. She crossed the room, a growing lump closing off her throat. Slowly she reached out and touched the delicate *yellow* rose petals. There was a card, and with a shaky hand she slipped it out of the small envelope.

The note was lean. Ry had simply signed his name.

The shrink had told him living in the past was manic. Suicidal, even. But Ry had argued the point. He'd tried to move forward and what he'd realized was that without Margo, life meant nothing. So he'd managed to stay sane another way—the answer wasn't learning to live without her, it was learning to live with her in a new way.

At that moment the tide had turned. He stopped drinking, and he'd stopped taking the pills, a dozen kinds for every mood. Then he'd designed a schedule for himself. He'd gotten back into top-notch physical shape, and he'd gotten busy shopping for a house. Next, he'd arranged his work schedule so he could have three evenings a week to spend at the Toucan with the woman he loved.

It was amazing what your mind could create with a little prompting. Each night Ry entered the Toucan he had imagined that Margo had invited him and that the songs she chose to sing were sung solely to him. Later, when he returned home, he furthered his fantasy by reliving the intimacy they had shared in that short month before his job had destroyed their happiness. In truth, his new life had been far better therapy than any damn pills, more soothing and satisfying than alcohol or warm milk. And it had been something perfectly safe as long as he stuck to the one rule he'd designed to keep him grounded. That rule had been distance—he would have absolutely no physical or verbal contact with Margo.

The shrink had called it insane; Ry had called it staying alive. Only now he knew that alive and living were two entirely different things. For two years he'd just been existing—last night was the first time he'd really lived since he'd walked out of Margo's life. Last night had made him realize something else, too—Margo had been just existing, too.

To say he wanted Margo back in his life was an understatement. He wanted to wake up next to her every morning. He wanted to kiss her anytime he felt like it. He wanted to take her to dinner and to the grocery store. He wanted to shop for vegetables with her and he wanted the choose wine together, toilet paper and toothpaste. He didn't care what, as long as they did it together. And he wanted to juggle every day for the rest of his life around seeing her and loving her.

Ry blinked out of his musing. He was standing in the file room at the stationhouse, his hand poised, ready to resurrect an old ghost. He pulled open the file and searched for the name that would forever be emblazoned in his mind.

"Banker's hours?"

Ry turned to see Clide saunter in just as he curled his fingers around Koch Menaro's file. "Hey, how's it going, Chief?"

"That's what I'd like to know. You haven't been to the lab yet this morning. What gives, Ry? You're usually so damn anxious to move forward on a case that you're standing on Archie's heels gnawing on his collarbone."

"I take it Archie's run the blood samples."

"He found three separate blood types. What do you make of that?"

Ry nodded. "I figured."

"You knew there was someone other than Mickey on the pier that night?"

"I knew."

"Why do I get the feeling you know more than you're saying, Ry? What gives?"

"You know me, Clide, I don't like to point a finger until I'm 99 percent sure."

"There's been plenty of times when all we had to go on was your reliable hunch. I've never complained."

That was true enough, but not this time, Ry wanted to say. There was no way he would tie Margo and Blu to the blood samples without solid proof, and maybe not even then. He let his hand drop as soon as he realized Clide was stretching his neck to read the name on the file. But he wasn't quick enough.

"What the hell are you doing with that?" Clide's brows lifted halfway up his forehead. "I thought we agreed—"

"*You* agreed we would forget about him. I didn't. How could I?"

"Koch is in hell, Ry. In a roundabout way, that is—in hell hanging around, is how I like to think of him. A smear here and a smudge over there."

"Not funny, Clide."

"When a body goes poof it takes on a new shape. But dead is dead, and Koch has been dead for two long years."

"You decided he was dead, I didn't." The bitterness in Ry's voice told the story—he was still too damn sensitive about the subject to be objective. But then what did Clide expect? It was Ry, along with three others who had made the ultimate sacrifice. Actually it was the other cops who had suffered the most. Ry had decided to cut his losses quickly instead of gambling with his loved one's life. And it had paid off—Koch Menaro had never known Margo ever existed. That's why she was still alive today.

"Dammit, Ry, I don't need you going wacko on me in the middle of this case. Why the hell are you going over this now? I thought you had settled things. You're off the booze and pills. You're sleeping, right?"

"I'm sleeping."

Clide sighed in relief.

"There's a big difference between living and existing, Clide."

"What the hell is that supposed to mean?"

"It means I want my old life back."

Ry knew that Clide understood what he was saying. His boss and Goddard Reese were the only two men who knew why he'd given up Margo and how low he'd sunk afterward. Only a select few at the precinct, on a need-to-know basis, had ever been informed about Koch Menaro and his vendetta against the Eighth District, and with good reason. News of Koch could have started an all-out panic at the precinct. As it was the department hadn't taken Koch seriously until he'd killed a police officer's wife on her way home from the grocery store, another officer's twin brother and the teenage daughter of a thirty-five-year veteran ready for retirement.

"Koch is dead," Clide said again.

Ry wanted to believe that, but, without any solid proof, he'd been left to wonder if the nightmare was really over. Closure was all he'd ever wanted, closure and the certainty that Margo would live to a ripe old age.

"Ry, you're making me nervous."

"I'm all right," he insisted. "The truth is…" Ry stopped himself. Just how much should he tell his boss?

"The truth is what?" Clide's eyebrows were climbing again.

"I've been in contact with Margo."

Clide swore. "I thought you said you weren't ready to do that. I thought you said if we didn't come up with a body, then—"

"I know what I said," Ry interrupted. "I still feel the same way, or at least I thought I did until a few days ago."

"I still can't give you a body! Either you're going to have to be able to live with that and face Margo with the truth, or live with things the way they are."

"Was I wrong to want a damn body, Clide? Was I wrong to want Koch on a slab, reconstructed with a little glue so I could see that bastard's face and know it was over?"

"A body would have been nice, and you're not the only one who wanted satisfaction. But the others accepted what they couldn't change and got on with their lives." Clide put his hand on Ry's shoulder. "Koch is dead. I don't know how many times I can say it to make you believe what I know in my heart to be true. If it wasn't true, Koch would be out there laughing at us and terrorizing the hell out of the people we love."

Ry jammed the folder back into the file drawer and slammed it shut. "I want back what he took from me, Clide. That's all."

"Okay." Clide raised his hands in understanding. "But can't this wait until after you've brought in Mickey's killer? This is a high-profile case, Ry. The news media is just waiting for us to screw something up so they can feed our fried butts to those insensitive jackasses upstairs. We can't afford to make a mistake right now. I need your full attention on this. I need you clear-headed and thinking straight. You've already kept Margo at arm's length for two years, what can another few weeks matter? A month? Two at the most?"

Ry turned to face Clide once more. "That would be the logical move, but I think I've got an eyewitness in the Burelly case."

"You do? Why the hell didn't you say…" Clide swore. "Wait a minute. You said you've seen Margo. Does that mean… Is she… Oh, hell. Don't tell me your eyewitness is Margo duFray."

"Okay, I won't tell you it's Margo."

Clide's face drained of color. "I'm going to have to pull you off the case, Ry. You know that."

"This is my case, dammit!" Ry was instantly furious. "Mine, Clide. If you turn it over to someone else it'll set you back days, weeks. Worse, what I've got so far will disappear."

"Blackmail! You think you can blackmail this department. Me!"

Ry pulled his badge from his pocket. "You want this?"

Clide swore. "See, already you're acting like a fool. What the hell am I supposed to do? You're my best detective when you're thinking straight, but we both know you have a hard time doing that when that little lady fits herself in the middle of your business."

"That's not fair, Clide."

"Life's not fair, son."

"You owe me, Clide. I didn't have to tell you that Margo could be my eyewitness. I didn't have to tell you a damn thing."

"No, you didn't." Clide sighed. "Okay, this is how we're going to handle this. You pick up that lab report from Archie and meet me in my office. We'll go over everything you've got so far, then, depending on your answers to my questions, I'll make my decision. I'll expect you in front of my desk in fifteen minutes."

It was closer to an hour before Ry opened the door to his boss's office and found Clide on the phone.

"Another body!" Clide reached for his antacid as Ry seated himself in front of his desk. "Holy hell. Where? I'll send my man down there pronto."

When Clide hung up, he popped the cap on his antacid bottle and tilted his head back. Ry lost count of the number of tablets that tumbled forward. "Another body?" he asked.

"Somebody came across a floater. Some fisherman in Algiers called it in. The victim's male, found him halfway between River Bay and DuBay Pier. You think he's got something to do with your case?"

"Is it still my case?" Ry asked.

"Harvey was waiting in my office when I got back from talking to you in the file room. The boys upstairs want this case wrapped up. I can't afford to reassign, not and keep the deadline they gave me."

"Which is?"

"You got four days to turn something up."

"Okay. Did you get an approximate age on our floater? Is he black or white?"

"White. No age."

Ry came to his feet, anxious to get down to the pier. At the door, his hand poised on the doorknob, he said, "Thanks, Clide. You won't regret this."

"If I do, I'll see you cleaning toilets at the morgue."

Ry had never been relieved before when he'd viewed a corpse. Today, however, seeing the floater and not being able to recognize him gave him cause to let out a deep sigh of relief.

He dropped the covering back over the dead body and stood. Pulling a notepad out of his pocket, he strolled toward the fisherman who had found the victim. The local man, a recreational fisherman, couldn't tell him much. He'd been heading out in his boat early and spotted the body floating face-down, halfway under the dock.

A few questions later, and Ry took the man's name, address and sent him on his way. Then he returned to the body. Kneeling, he examined the corpse. The man's face was distorted and swollen, his body bloated, but not overly. He hadn't been in the water all that long from the looks of him. Ry figured ten or twelve hours max. One shot had done the trick—a single, small-caliber entry wound just above his right eye. He was wearing a suit and tie, fairly new shoes, and a better-than-average watch on his wrist. He had bruised knuckles to go along with the bruises on his face, signs that he'd been engaged in a fight sometime before or during his death. He was a big man, well over six foot and muscular, not the kind of man who would go down easily.

After Ry had inventoried the man's appearance, he added a number of questions like he always did to the bottom of his note pad. Minutes later, he turned his attention on the crowd who had gathered. He scanned the faces, hoping he'd get lucky and Blu duFray would be among them. Not surprised when he wasn't, Ry began to search for the big fellow, Brodie Hewitt. It suddenly dawned on him in the midst of his search that there was an unusual number of duFray Devils standing around.

Ry checked his watch and found it well past eight. The fishing business started early; some boats were moving before sunrise. The duFray Devils—Blu's crew—were the early-bird fleet, the first boats to slip away from the docks and head through the canal to the Gulf. But not today. Why?

Ry headed toward the collected crowd. "Can anyone tell me where I might find Blu duFray or Brodie Hewitt this morning?"

The crew side-glanced each other, shrugged their shoulders and shook their heads. Finally a thin man in his sixties—a man Ry thought he recognized— missing his front teeth, stepped forward.

"Name's Pike, Detective. We don't know where Blu is, but Brodie's been stayin' on Blu's cruiser for the past two days. It's long past the hour we should be out on the water, but Brodie ain't showed up."

The moment the man gave his name, Ry knew why he had recognized him. Pike duFray was Margo's uncle. "Maybe he's sleeping off a hang- over somewhere," Ry said, remembering Hewitt's taste for liquor.

"He ain't sleeping late. Leastwise, not on the cruiser. I checked. For a minute, when they hauled that body out of the river I thought it was—"

"Hewitt?" Ry arched a brow. "Would there be a reason why you'd think that?"

Pike hesitated, then said, "That fellow was big. Big like Brodie. That and the late hour. We never leave port this late."

"Maybe Hewitt decided to take the day off," Ry suggested.

The older man shook his head. "Brodie's no slouch. Not even when Blu's away. We work same as any other day. Sometimes longer."

"And Blu's away?"

"He didn't work yesterday."

"You know where I can find him?"

Pike shrugged. "Can't say."

"Can't?"

"Don't know," he amended.

Ry scanned the faces of the seasoned crew. "Any of you know different? Got something to add?"

Their answer was random head shaking with blank looks.

Ry left the duFray Devils standing dockside and walked a few blocks to where the *Nightwing* rode the calm tide at River Bay. He was just about to board when he heard footsteps behind him. He turned to see Pike eyeing him.

"Came to have a few more words with you, Detective."

"Forget something?" Ry asked.

Pike shot his hands into the pockets of his baggy trousers, driving them further down his narrow hips. "I boarded her 'bout an hour ago. Thought Brodie was sick or somethin'. There's no sign of him, but it looks like he had some uninvited company before mornin'. I found blood topside near the stern. Lots of it. Didn't want to mention it in front of the boys. They're worried enough about keepin' their paychecks rollin' regular. I don't much care for you, and I'm sure you know why, so helpin' you ain't why I'm doin' this. Brodie's a friend of mine. Blu's family. Margo's the only niece I got."

Ry nodded. "I'll need you to come downtown and make a statement. If this is the crime scene, I'm authorized to impound the boat."

"That won't make Blu happy." Pike shrugged. "But if it'll turn up Brodie, I guess Blu would be willin' to lend it to you for a day or two. Long as you treat her like she was your own."

Within the hour, Ry had ordered the *Nightwing* impounded, then asked Pike to take a ride downtown with him. At the precinct he recorded Pike's answers to his pointed questions, most of them repeats from their conversation on the waterfront, and when they were finished, he handed the typed copy to Pike and had him read the statement. "If it's what you said, sign it."

Margo's uncle scanned the paper, then scratched his signature on it. He stood ready to leave. Ry said, "I appreciate you coming down, Pike."

"I didn't do it for you. Still gnaws at my guts what you did to our little girl. Margo's special. She deserved better than she got from you."

"I agree," Ry admitted. "At the time that's why I set her free."

Pike frowned at that, then started to leave. Turning back, he muttered, "Must have somethin' to do with being Texan. Ain't met one yet that made much sense."

By midday, Ry made a call to Jackson to update him on what he'd found in Algiers, and check on Margo. Jackson informed him that he'd heard about the floater at DuBay Pier, and so had Margo. He explained that he and Margo were eating lunch at the kitchen table, listening to the radio, when it came over the noon news. He also told Ry that since then she'd been a wreck. She'd also tried to escape twice.

"Don't let her out of your sight," Ry insisted. "She'll likely try and skip on you again. I can't get back there for a few hours, so hang close to her. Don't tell her I called, and don't talk about the floater. Did she use the phone?"

"Yeah, she called Hewitt a half dozen times, but he's not picking up."

Ry hung up the phone and eased back in his chair. Normally he was a patient man when it came to dissecting his cases. He knew that time always had a way of adding insight, and that trying too hard sometimes worked against you. But today he wasn't feeling at all patient with the situation. He wanted answers, and Margo might not know all of them, but he suspected she knew enough to turn the tide.

Maybe after last night she would be willing to trust him. What was he saying? Did he think one night in his bed would erase the humiliation he'd caused her and she'd simply wipe the slate clean? No, he knew better than that. Still, if he could gain her trust—convince her she could depend on him like in the old days. And if he could find a way to tell her the truth about Koch without making things worse....

Then, too, maybe a fairy would appear and kiss his butt.

Chapter 8

A man was dead and they'd found his body in the river near DuBay Pier. The first time Margo heard it she was sitting at the kitchen table with Jackson. He'd convinced her he could cook, and she'd let him fix her lunch. The next time she'd heard it she was pacing the floor in Ry's bedroom chewing on her lower lip.

The news report said the body had been spotted early morning, a white male in his twenties. Margo had tried to call Brodie with no luck, then she'd swallowed her pride and called the precinct and asked to speak to Detective Archard. When she couldn't reach Ry, she'd started to cry. Minutes later she'd attempted a reckless escape that had proven to be futile—Jackson Ward was as shrewd as Ry, and he'd anticipated her plan, right down to which door she would use and which direction she'd head. She'd made a second attempt a few hours later, but as she'd slipped through the hole in the hedge she'd run straight into Jackson's muscled chest.

Now, hours later, Margo was fast falling apart. Her eyes were swollen from hours of crying, and her head pounded like a too tightly wound clock. She had blisters on her heels from pacing, and her chewed lip was bleeding. Internally her frustration had turned into a melting pot of acid in the pit of her stomach. *Sick* couldn't begin to describe how miserable she felt.

She couldn't understand why Ry hadn't called her back or come home. She'd left him a dozen messages at the precinct. Surely he'd gotten at least one of them.

Maybe if she started the house on fire that would get someone's attention. She certainly wasn't getting anywhere pacing or crying. As she contemplated searching the kitchen for matches, she heard Ry's Blazer drive up. Matches forgotten, Margo raced through the back door and nearly toppled Jackson out of the hammock as he swung his long legs to the floor. Ignoring his verbal displeasure, she watched Ry climb out of the vehicle.

Past anxious, she yelled, "Where the hell have you been?" Not giving him time to answer, she added, "Didn't you get any of my messages?" It was then she noticed his sober expression, and she snapped her mouth shut.

"I got the messages," he said, strolling across the yard. "I wanted to see you in person."

Margo's stomach clenched. "Tell me, damn you. Tell me who it was." He climbed the steps with slow deliberation. "Stick around, Jackson. There's some things we need to talk over. But later, okay."

"It's Blu, isn't it?" Panic engulfed Margo, and her imagination ran wild. She could see her brother's face just before they dove into the water, hear his wonderful deep voice. "Tell me. Tell me, damn you!"

Margo was vaguely aware that Jackson had wandered down the steps and disappeared. Her throat froze up, and her tongue thickened as Ry took Jackson's place on the veranda. She shook her head, tried to speak. When nothing came out, she grabbed the front of Ry's shirt and balled it into her fist. "I'm sick of waiting. I want to know what's happened to my brother!"

He put his arm around her and pulled her close, an action that made Margo's blood run cold—he had horrible news to tell her. She was right—the body they had recovered was Blu's body. Oh, God! Oh, *God!*

At that moment all Margo's strength drained from her body and she sagged against Ry's chest. He wrapped his arm around her and guided her back into the house. "Come on, baby, sit down." He pushed her gently onto a chair at the kitchen table, then knelt in front of her.

Margo felt her sanity slip. She started crying again. "Please not Blu. Tell me they didn't kill him, Ry. Tell me it's all been a terrible mistake."

Her body started to shake, and to keep from totally losing control, she wrapped her arms around herself. It was what she had feared all day, but she'd tried to convince herself that Blu was too smart to let something like this happen. Her brother was tough as shoe leather and twice as durable. He couldn't be dead.

Ry gripped her arms and shook her a little. "Did you hear me? I said, tell me what you know, baby. Tell me who *they* are and why they were after Blu. If I'm going to be any good to you, I have to know what happened in Algiers the other night. Blu would want you to tell me, baby. He's not here to help so you're going to have to do it for him."

He's not here to help. Margo cried harder.

"I know it's hard for you, baby, but try. The sooner I know what I'm up against, the better."

She knew Ry was right. And she agreed—Blu would want her to tell the police what she knew. There was no reason not to now. She should have told Ry everything sooner. Maybe then...

More crying.

"Blu called me a few nights ago and asked me to meet him. He said he needed some pictures taken." She sniffed and rubbed her eyes. "He called it an *exchange*. He said, 'I want pictures of the exchange, Chili.'" Margo started to cry in earnest. "He loved calling me that. It's the reason I decided to use it as my stage name."

"I know, baby. Keep going."

"I don't know what they were exchanging. I didn't ask. But it must have been that key you found in my pocket. Blu gave it to me just before we dove into the river."

"Back up and explain where you were when this happened."

"I was in the alley behind Cruger's Bar taking pictures when I heard the first two shots." Margo squeezed her eyes shut for a moment remembering.

"Margo... Come on, baby. I need to know all of it."

She blinked open her eyes. "The shots scared me, and I dropped the camera and it broke. The man with Blu was lying on the pier, and…I heard another shot." Tears streamed down Margo's cheeks. "That's when I panicked and ran."

"Ran?"

"Yes, to warn Blu to get off the pier."

"You what… You headed into the line of fire?"

Confused by the sudden harshness in Ry's voice, Margo watched him jerk to his feet. "I can't believe you would do something so damn stupid! A crazy stunt like that could have cost you your life!" His face turned red with anger. Furious, his hand shot out and he drove his fist into the yellow wall, knocking the yellow clock to the floor and breaking it into pieces. "How dare Blu put you in that kind of position? When I find that arrogant little bastard brother of yours I'm going to kill him for real!" he roared.

Margo was sure she had heard wrong. Slowly she came to her feet. "Ry, you just—"

The look he gave her said it all. Instant relief swept over Margo, then instant outrage. "You lying bastard! You low-life snake! Disgusting worm!" She raised her fist.

Ry caught her arm. "Easy, baby. Hear me out."

"How dare you!" She tried to break free, but he wouldn't let her go.

"Settle down, Margo. You're going to break open those damn stitches if you're not careful."

"To hell with the stitches! To hell with you!" He had purposely made her think that Blu was dead to glean information from her. How could he do something so despicable? So cruel?

"I'm trying to help you, dammit. And Blu, too. It might not look that way right now, but—"

"It sure as hell doesn't." Margo continued to fight him. Succeeding in twisting free, she hauled back and slapped him hard across the face. His head snapped back, her handprint remaining as a stinging reminder of the force behind her anger.

Within seconds he had wrestled her back into his arms. This time imprisoning her against his body. "Okay, I deserved that. But you've got to trust me now."

"Ha!"

"Listen to me, dammit! We've got to stop playing games with each other. I don't deserve your trust, but right now I need it. Yes, dammit, I lied. I pretended the stiff was Blu. It was the best I could do on short notice. I'm running out of time, and frankly so is Blu."

Margo felt sick and empty. She would never forgive Ry for his calculated deception. It was the ultimate betrayal. "Let go of me. I don't want you touching me. I don't want you in the same room with me."

He let her go and she took a step back. "Margo…"

"Go to hell."

"Not before I solve this case. Whether you believe it or not I care about you. You're smack in the middle of my case, yes, but that's not what this is about. It's about keeping you safe, and finding Blu alive."

"And I'm supposed to believe that?" Margo held up her hand, not wanting to hear another lie. "No more. I won't hear any more."

"That's where you're wrong, baby. You're going to hear plenty more."

"I hate you!" She screamed, then reached out and knocked the dozen long-stem roses off the table in one angry, reckless motion. The vase crashed to the floor, the water spilling and the roses scattering.

"You can hate me all you want," he offered, standing tall in the midst of her fury, "but you're still going to listen to what I have to say." Stepping over the roses, he stalked her.

"Two men are dead, and Brodie Hewitt's missing. If you think I'm going to sit back and watch you be the next victim you're crazy."

Cornered, with no place to go, Margo had to listen. "Brodie's missing?" She felt her world tilt once more. "How do you know that? How can I believe you?"

"Pike. He came to the precinct and gave a statement. You can read it if you need to be convinced. The way I see it, both Blu and Brodie are up to their necks in something, and the only one who seems to give a damn about that right now is me."

"I give a damn!"

"Then I suggest you pull yourself together and stop seeing me as the enemy. Or do you hate me more than you love Blu?"

She was right, Ry thought, he was a low-life snake, a selfish bastard who... Who would do whatever he had to, to keep her safe. Hadn't he proven that two years ago? Margo just didn't know who she was dealing with; he was the man who loved her, dammit! The man who had sacrificed everything to keep her alive and healthy. Only, she didn't know that. She had no idea how he felt about her, or the reason behind his leaving her two years ago.

Seeing Margo hysterical and in tears had ripped his heart in two. She would never know how hard it had been to stand there and pretend that Blu was dead. But what he'd told her afterward was pure truth; Blu and Brodie were in the middle of something deadly, and could easily be killed, that is if they weren't dead already.

All he needed was another damn body pulled from the river and...

Ry knelt to clean up the mess on the floor. He tried to rescue the roses, but in the end he tossed them in the garbage. When he had finished, he sank onto the chair at the kitchen table and lowered his head into his hands. The bottom line was Margo had to resign herself to the facts. She might hate him and hate working with him, but they were in this thing together for the long haul, like it or not.

Yes, he'd lied. But he hadn't planned on deceiving her, not until he'd talked to the dispatcher the last time and had listened to Margo's bizarre state of mind. At that moment, he had known just what buttons to push to get her to talk; after all, Margo cared for Blu with a passion that few siblings ever experienced. Yes, he was jealous of her fierce loyalty to her brother, but in this case he had used that loyalty to his advantage; Margo's weakness had become her Achilles' heel. A vulnerability he could use because he knew it would guarantee results.

Ry checked his watch. She'd been upstairs a long hour. In that time he had filled Jackson in on the situation, then sent his partner out to search for Goddard Reese. God was good about checking in, and he hadn't.

His thoughts back on Margo, Ry wondered if she had cooled down any. If he went upstairs would they talk like two civilized adults, or would she throw something at him and demand he leave?

Ry stood, then slowly walked through the kitchen. He paused at the bottom of the stairs. Was he completely crazy to think that maybe after all this they still stood a chance?

He climbed the stairs and lingered a moment at his bedroom door with his hand poised on the knob. Before she had left him standing in the kitchen, she had given him one last look. The hate in her beautiful eyes had burned straight through to his soul. Would it still be there?

He could appreciate her anger, and maybe even live with her hate if in the end she was safe. Hell, all he'd ever wanted was for her to be alive and happy.

Ry opened the door and found Margo standing at the window. The plated moon had cast her heavenly curves in shadow, and the sight sent his blood pumping hard and fast. The day's sultry heat hadn't let up, and the room felt shut up and close. He moved to the air conditioner and turned it on. The sound made her turn around.

He knew he would have to be the one to initiate the conversation. "So what's it going to be, baby? Are we partners, or do I put you in protective custody until this case is solved?"

On hearing his radical solution, her chin rose a fraction. "Protective custody? Why?"

"Because I can't do my job and worry about where you are every minute of the day."

"And if I say yes and tell you what I know, I can go home?"

"You don't have a home, remember?"

"I do so," she hissed.

"The answer's no. I won't let you leave here. I've got plenty of room. Once we've caught the people responsible for the killings, then we can—"

"There's no 'we,' Detective Archard."

Ry started over. "Okay, once *I've* apprehended the criminals, you can go where you want. How's that?"

"I'm not afraid. This isn't about me."

"You're wrong about that." Ry took a step closer. "This involves anyone who knows anything about that night. And you were there. I don't think you're their primary target, but I don't want you getting in the way of another stray bullet meant for Blu."

"I don't think that's your call, Detective Archard. If I'm willing to take a bullet meant for my brother, that's my business."

"You're crazy if you think I would stand by and let that happen. Last night—"

"Was just sex. We both agreed."

"Last night was more than just sex and we both know it. If you'd be honest, you'd admit at least that much."

"Oh, please. You're chastising me about being honest."

"I care about you."

"It's painfully clear what you care about, Ry, and

it has nothing to do with me, and everything to do with that damn job of yours.''

''That's not fair. This just happens to be my case, but that—''

She cut him off. ''I made a bad choice coming here the other night, and I'm sorry about that. You don't know just how sorry. But I would never have come if Blu hadn't been so insistent. So you see, it wasn't my idea. In fact, I refused at first, and then—''

''Wait a minute. It was Blu's idea you come here? When did he suggest that?''

She stubbornly hesitated.

''Margo, if you ever hope to get out of this house before Christmas, you had better start talking.'' Ry nailed her with hard eyes and a determined set to his jaw. ''I mean it. You're not leaving here the way things stand. The sooner I wrap up this case, the sooner you'll be free to leave. Not a minute sooner.''

A long minute passed before she relented. ''We were on the pier, Blu and me. The cop was dead. By the way, I didn't know he was a cop until later when you told me. Anyway, the men who shot him suddenly came out from wherever they'd been hiding and started toward the pier. Blu said we needed to dive into the river to get away. I didn't want to. He'd been shot in the leg, me in the arm. You know how I feel about water. I'm not the world's greatest swimmer. I started to argue, but Blu wouldn't listen. He said once I got away, I should swim to the *Nightwing* and have Brodie bring me here. He said no one would think to look for me in your home. I rejected the idea at first, then decided he was right.''

Ry thought a minute. It didn't make sense, Blu suggesting Margo come to him, not unless... Unless Blu knew Margo was in serious danger and he wouldn't be able to protect her. And Ry suspected Blu knew something else, too. He knew the incident on the pier was just the beginning—the beginning of something bigger.

One thing Ry had never questioned was Blu's love for his sister. Even though he could be reckless as hell, Blu had taken on the male role in the duFray household after Carl had died. He'd watched over Margo like a possessive father, and he'd made sure the fish market remained on solid footing to keep his mother busy and financially independent.

So what was Blu trying to tell him? Ry wanted to know. What was in front of his eyes that he still couldn't see?

"What about the key I found in your pocket? Did Blu say anything about the key?"

She shook her head. "No."

"Has Blu introduced you to anyone lately? Some new face, a special friend? Think, Margo. Have there been any new faces hanging around Blu? Did he mention a lucky opportunity he'd fallen on? Something that would net him a big windfall?"

"No! I've already told you, I don't know. There's nothing I can tell you."

"You're sure?"

"Yes, dammit! Blu never talked business to me except to assure me that he wasn't going to let Daddy's fishing fleet fall apart. I know you think Blu is irresponsible, but he's not. He's got over thirty men working for him. They need regular paychecks. The repairs on the boats are a weekly prob-

lem. And then there's Mama to consider. Her medical insurance eats up over half of the fish market's
profits.'' She took a long-overdue breath. ''I don't
need to go on, do I? I've never hidden how much I
admire and love my brother. He doesn't say one
thing, then do another. What you see is what you
get, as they say.''

What she was saying was that Blu was everything
he wasn't. It was hard to swallow, but the truth often
is, when it's labeling you the scum of the earth and
your position is lower than the bottom of the heap.

Ry dug the key out of his pocket. ''So Blu didn't
say anything specific about this key?''

''No! He joked that it had something to do with
a treasure map, but...'' Her eyes suddenly went
wide. ''And he said to give it to you if he didn't
show up in a couple of days. Oh, God! How could
I have forgotten that part?''

Now they were getting somewhere. ''A treasure
map? You're sure he said map?''

''Yes.'' She sank into the paisley chair. ''I don't
think he said anything else. But, my God, what if
I'm forgetting something else? What if I've dismissed something really important?''

''Take it easy.'' Ry walked over to the bed and
sat on the edge facing her. ''Did Brodie say anything
that night? Did he imply he knew what was going
on?''

''I think he knew something because Blu said
Brodie had no doubt heard the shot and would know
things had gone to hell. Then, once I was on the
Nightwing, and I told him what happened and where
Blu said I should go, he didn't argue. He didn't want
to leave me, but he also seemed anxious to find Blu.

Almost as if he knew where he might be, or maybe he was just as worried as I was.''

"How do you know that?"

"I don't, for sure. Brodie was upset about my arm, but he seemed more together that night. Almost like he had half expected something to go wrong and had known what to do just in case."

"He wasn't drinking, then?"

"No. He does enjoy his liquor, but he wasn't drinking that night."

Ry didn't say it, but he wondered if Hewitt was more mixed up in this than he first figured. He was supposed to be Blu's friend, Margo's love interest. Was Brodie sincere, or did he have an agenda all his own?"

"You said you came here by cab? Now you say Brodie brought you. Which is it?"

"Brodie brought me."

"Then he went back to Algiers to search for Blu?"

"Yes."

Ry shook his head. "I still can't believe he just left you with a bullet hole in your arm."

"We were both worried about Blu," she snapped. "I knew I would be fine. The wound wasn't serious. He knew that, too. Don't you dare find fault with Brodie."

Ry didn't want to rile her. A defensive Margo would likely stop talking. They were making progress. He didn't need her getting stubborn on him and clamming up. "So why do you suppose Blu wanted the photos?"

"I have no idea." She lowered her eyes and stared at her hands folded in her lap. "I love my brother, but I'm not a fool, Ry. I know he gambles to keep the cash flow moving. I know he's done some other things, too. Things some people would condemn him for." She glared at him, letting Ry know she thought he was one of the "some people."

"I know he walks a narrow line, baby."

"He would never kill a cop, Ry. He wouldn't go that far for a buck!"

"No, I don't think he would, either. But he's worked for men that are capable of doing that and more." Ry wasn't sure just how much to tell Margo, how much she would accept from him. He didn't need to drive a deeper wedge between them, it was already halfway to hell. But maybe the truth was the only way to reach her. "Margo, listen—"

"I know what you're going to say. Don't bother."

"I have to. Blu might be your brother, but I know for a fact that he's also hired muscle for at least one loan shark in town. Patch Pollaro pays Blu to keep his clients honest and on time. There might be others, too."

He saw her physically stiffen, then she looked away. "I thought it was something like that. I've seen his hands, his knuckles are often bruised and swollen. I've asked him about it a few times. He blamed it on working on the boats."

"I'm not condemning him, Margo."

"Aren't you?" She locked eyes with him. "You've always disliked my brother."

"We've had our differences," Ry agreed, "but I've never gone after him. Honest, baby, I don't want him on the wrong side in this."

"Sure, and I'm supposed to believe that."

Ry stood, knowing anything he said to vindicate

himself right now would be useless. He took her earlier stance at the window. "Could be Blu saw something he shouldn't have. Could be he's a victim in this."

"You don't really believe that."

No, he didn't, but there was a small chance. He glanced over his shoulder to see that she was on her feet waiting for him to vindicate her brother. "Blu, a victim, seems highly unlikely. Your brother is damn resourceful. But stranger things have happened."

"And Brodie? Where do you think he is right now?"

The worry in her eyes, in her voice, was to be expected, but Ry found himself turning jealous, anyway. "Pike said Brodie was staying on the *Nightwing*. We found blood on deck and evidence of a struggle."

"Blood on the *Nightwing*! Why didn't you tell me this before?"

"Because you didn't give me a chance. My guess is it's blood from the dead guy we pulled from the river, but the lab will make that call. I had the *Nightwing* impounded for that reason. I'm thinking whoever is hunting Blu boarded the *Nightwing* last night with the intention of getting some answers from Brodie. They fought, and Brodie blew the man's head off."

"No way! Brodie wouldn't kill anyone."

"Not even to save himself?"

"If that's what happened, where is he now?"

She began to worry her lip, and it was all Ry could do to stand there and watch her concern for another man. For a long time he had watched Hewitt come and go at the Toucan, but he had never wanted to believe the rumors. They were just friends, he'd told himself, that was it.

Don't be jealous, he warned himself. Don't let those feelings get in the way. Not now.

"Hewitt could be on the run," he suggested. "Or maybe he's hooked up with Blu. Take your pick. It could have happened ten different ways. The dead guy might not even be a part of this. He could have been dumped."

He watched her bury her face in her hands. "I can't stand this waiting. We have to do something."

"We are. And if you want to help, tell me everything again, just like it happened. Take it from when you heard the shots and raced to the pier. Go through it step by step. Maybe there's something more you've forgotten."

"I don't like remembering that night. I heard shots, saw the man Blu was talking to drop over dead, and I ran."

"To the pier."

The outrage in his voice set her off. "Yes. Yes, to the pier! That's where Blu was, and that's where I wanted to be at that moment."

Ry still had a hard time imagining Margo racing onto that pier. The gun that had taken Mickey out had been an AK-47, for God's sake. She could have died so easily. Every time he thought about it, his stomach knotted.

"Before I got to him, he went down," she was saying. "I thought he was dead, and I... He started cussing then, and when I heard it I was so happy. I started to run toward him again, and that's when he saw me and started yelling, ordering me to jump off the pier into the water. I heard another shot, then another. I don't remember much after I was hit. Blu hauled me over the dead cop and covered me with his own body. That's when my ribs were bruised. He checked my arm to see how bad I was hit, then gave me the key. I was in the water swimming for the *Nightwing* minutes later. And Blu—''

She started to cry. "I don't remember him letting go of my hand. I heard more shots. Splashing. I think he drew them away from me to give me time to get away. The river was so black and so cold.''

Again Ry could picture her running on the pier with bullets flying, could envision the moment she was shot, her swimming the river alone in the dead of night. The whole scene made him feel as if his insides were being ripped out of him through a pinhole. He gritted his teeth, wanted to go to her, to pull her into his arms and hold her. He wanted to promise her that nothing like that would ever happen again.

But it would be a false promise, Ry realized. Yes, he could try his best to keep her safe, happy, but he wasn't God. And that's what Clide had been telling him for two years—*Life has no guarantees,* he'd said at least once a week. *It's not fair, or always pretty. We live each day the best we can. The reward is sharing those days with someone special.*

"I have to do something,'' she said suddenly. "Maybe if you used me as bait in some way. Maybe if I went back to my apartment and they showed up and—''

"No! I don't even know who these people are, but I damn sure know what they're capable of. Using you as bait is out of the question. You're here with Jackson during the day and me at night until this case it solved." Ry ended the discussion by standing. As he walked past her, he said, "I'm going downstairs to fix us a late supper."

"I'm not hungry."

"You need food."

"I need Blu!"

Ry swore but kept moving to the door. "Well I'm the only one here right now, baby, so you're going to have to settle for less, I guess."

He had just stepped into the hall when he heard a knock at the back door. He stopped dead in his tracks and glanced back at Margo. Sure she had heard the knock, too, he brought his finger to his lips to silence her.

The knock came again.

Ry moved quickly. He crossed the room, snared Margo by the arm and ushered her to the bed.

"What are you doing?"

"That's not Jackson. He wouldn't knock. Until I know who it is, I want you up here out of sight." He released her, then said, "I'm sorry, but I'm going to have to lock you up."

"Lock me up? What does that mean?"

He pulled his handcuffs from his pocket. "Understand, I need to know that you're going to be here when I get back. The way things stand between us, you giving me your word just doesn't seem like enough."

"Can you blame me?"

"No, that's why this is necessary."

"You're going to handcuff me to...to the bedpost?"

Ry followed her gaze. "The bedpost... Good

idea.'' Quickly he clamped the handcuff on her wrist, then around the bedpost. ''I won't be long,'' he promised, then hurried toward the door. Halfway there he stopped, then hurried back, pulled the navy satin pillow from beneath the covers and shredded it. Using a strip of satin, he gagged her. ''No noise,'' he said by way of justifying his actions, then hurried to answer the persistent knocking at the back door.

Chapter 9

Ry heard another knock as he stepped into the kitchen. He retrieved his second .38 Special, the one he kept stashed in the bread saver, then opened the door and shoved the gun into the face of Rose duFray.

Rose promptly gasped and nearly backed off the veranda. "My Lord!"

"Sorry," Ry swore, and lowered the gun.

"Gracious, Ryland. If that's how you greet all your guests, it's a wonder you have any company at all."

Ry stuffed the gun into the waistband of his jeans. "I thought you were someone else. I thought you were... Ah—never mind what I thought. What can I do for you, Mrs. duFray?"

"I know it's late, and I apologize for that. I just didn't know who else to turn to, Ryland. Do you mind if I come in for a minute?"

Rose didn't give Ry a chance to answer. She nudged past him and entered his kitchen, her gaze taking in the layout with keen interest. "My, this is sure something. So much room, and so bright. You must like yellow. I haven't seen so much of one color in a single room ever. Look there, you've even got a yellow sink."

Ry looked around the room, his gaze falling on all the yellow. Pretty much everything that was available in the color yellow was in this room. Besides the bedroom, he spent the most time in this room. He supposed to someone who didn't understand his motivation, the room looked like a lemonade factory on Sunshine Boulevard. But there was a reason, a good reason why the room and everything in it was yellow—it was Margo's favorite color.

She was saying, "You could fit my entire kitchen and living room in here. Maybe my bathroom, too." She turned back and looked at Ry with a dozen questions brimming in her eyes. "Do you live here alone?"

"Yes."

"All this for one person?" She looked at him with one raised gray brow. "Most men want things simple. Especially if they live alone and work as much as you do. Do you entertain a lot?"

"No."

"Your family visit often?"

"No. My folks don't like to travel much, and my only brother keeps pretty busy on the ranch in Texas."

She studied the clean floor. "You got a... housekeeper?"

Ry grinned. Rose duFray wasn't thinking house-keeper at all, what she really wanted to know was if he had a female companion. He said, "Yes I do. She comes in once a week."

"Once a week, that's it?" She glanced toward the living room as if curious to see the rest of the house. Ry had no intention of giving her a guided tour. What would he say once they climbed the stairs and he opened his bedroom door? 'Oh, and this is the master bedroom, Mrs. duFray, and that there is your daughter gagged and chained to my bed. The colors in the room complement Margo's hair and eyes, don't you think?'

Ry shuddered at the thought. Hell, he could exchange gunfire in a damn shoot-out or run down a psycho, and yet Margo's mother could make him tongue-tied within a matter of seconds.

He looked toward the living room half expecting Margo to come through the door, dragging the bed-post behind her. The vision was as unkind as the bedroom tour and it spurred him into action. Ry caught Rose's arm before she made herself too com-fortable. "Why don't we sit outside? The house is stuffy tonight."

"Nonsense, it feels fine." She glanced down at his hand on her arm, and Ry quickly withdrew it. He watched her amble to the table and ease her slim body onto a chair. Cradling her handbag in her lap, she boldly assessed his appearance. "You look tired, Ryland. You need more sleep."

Sleep. Yes, he could use some sleep. In the past two days he'd had less than six hours. "Can I get you something? Lemonade, iced tea?"

"No, nothing, thank you."

Ry sat across from her and took inventory of Margo's mother. She looked the same as always, dressed in a serviceable skirt and lightweight blouse. Her style was as simple and straightforward as her mannerisms, and yet it couldn't and didn't hide her natural beauty. In her midfifties, Rose had survived the loss of her husband and the bills and burdens Carl had left behind. She was a hard worker with a mountain of faith in her children.

"So what did you want to talk about?" Ry asked, prepared to make this as quick as possible.

"It's Margo," Rose confessed. "She called me this morning. We talked only a few minutes. That was all right, she's busy, you know. But later I remembered I hadn't told her about my doctor's appointment tomorrow. Margo insists on knowing every little detail, so I tried to call her back. She was staying with a friend, so she said, but when I called Angie—her friend—she said Margo wasn't there. In fact, she claimed she hadn't seen my daughter in days. I called the Toucan and talked to that nice Mr. Bichon. He said Margo was still sick, and she had planned to take a few more days off. Now neither story makes any sense, Ryland. I went to Margo's apartment, and she didn't answer the door."

"I'm sure there's a simple explanation, Mrs. duFray."

She eyed Ry with a look that made him feel like she was trying to see inside his head. "And just what would that be, Ryland? Margo said she was helping out a friend, and the friend doesn't know it. Does this make sense to you?"

No, it didn't make sense, but Ry didn't think the

truth was going to make sense to Rose, either. Or help out her blood pressure.

"She didn't sound sick on the phone. Mr. Bichon said she was sick." Rose paused. "Maybe a little tired, now that I think on it, but I would have known if my daughter was sick. I would have heard it in her voice." She frowned. "My Margo doesn't lie, Ryland, so my gut tells me there's cause for alarm. Am I right?"

As far as Rose knew, he and Margo were still estranged. She probably didn't even know about the evenings he spent at the Toucan. If he was too eager to help, Rose might get suspicious. "Mrs. duFray, I don't know that I can answer that. Margo and I haven't—"

"Spoken in some time. Yes, I know." She reached out and patted his arm. "I know this is a little awkward for you, Ryland. Actually, if I could have found Blu this wouldn't have been necessary. He was my first choice naturally, only when I went down to the dock his boat was gone. Brodie's nowhere to be found, either. I tell you, Ryland, if I didn't know better, I'd say something strange is going on. And after that poor soul was pulled from the river this morning… Well, I just need to hear my daughter's voice."

"I'm sure Margo's fine, Mrs. duFray. Blu, too." Ry glanced toward the living room. When he looked back, Rose said, "Have I interrupted something? You seem a little nervous. I know it's late. I just assumed you were alone, but then that's an old woman's way of thinking, isn't it? You're too young to be spending your nights with Mickey Spillane." She chuckled at her own wit.

"No, I'm alone. I was just...I was doing some work in the study. Ah, a case. I was going over a case file and I..." God, Ry thought, he was stammering like a thief caught with the goods in his back pocket. No, the goods weren't in his back pocket, he reminded himself, but chained to his bedpost.

"You're such a nice boy, Ryland." Another pat on the arm. "I always thought you and Margo made such a good-looking couple. Well, never mind what I thought. What's important is what you thought. You and Margo, that is." She went silent for a moment, then said, "It was just so quick, you changing your mind."

"I never meant to hurt her," Ry said, sure the words were too little too late.

"I never believed what Pike said about you taking advantage of my Margo. I want you to know that, Ryland. Margo knew full well what could happen with an older man." Rose sighed. "Well, there's no sense crying over boiled-dry stew. I like Brodie well enough. I just don't see any sparks there, but..."

The silence that followed turned uncomfortably potent. Ry stood, in hopes that Rose would take the hint. But just as she came to her feet, a loud crash echoed from overhead. "What in heaven's name was that?"

"Nothing to worry about." Ry nearly bit his tongue off hurrying to explain. "I'm baby-sitting the neighbor's...ah, cat. She must have knocked something over upstairs."

Ry watched Rose set down her handbag on the table. "Get the broom, Ryland. I'll give you a hand before I go."

"No! Ah, I mean... It's not necessary. I'll clean

it up.'' Ry swung her handbag off the table and nearly took Rose's head off in the process. His hand on her back, he steered her to the door. ''I'm used to housework. A little broken glass is nothing.''

She stopped at the door and eyed him for a moment. ''If that's true, it's a sad waste a man as handsome as you never got married. These days a young woman would appreciate a man who isn't afraid to bend over and pick up his shorts.''

Ry nodded, cut her a hasty smile, then swung open the door and handed Rose her purse. ''I'll find Margo for you and tell her to give you a call. Will you be all right going home?''

''Of course. I carry pepper spray,'' Rose declared. ''Margo insists. And I always take a taxi. He's waiting out on the street. Are you sure I can't offer you a hand with the broom?''

''No. I'll take care of it. Good night, Mrs. du-Fray.''

''I don't imagine I'll get any sleep until my girl calls, so tell Margo not to worry about the time. I just need to hear her voice.''

''I'll tell her,'' Ry promised.

''Thank you, Ryland. You're such a good boy.''

''I didn't mean to break the lamp,'' Margo said the minute Ry removed the gag from her mouth. ''I was trying to slide this damn thing up the bedpost and I lost my balance. It's your fault. If you hadn't—''

''You didn't get cut, did you?''

Margo saw he was eyeing the broken glass around her bare feet. ''If I have, that's your fault, too.''

He swore, then pulled the cuff keys from his

pocket and released her. Before Margo could move, he lifted her off her feet and laid her on the bed. "Let me see."

"No!" Margo tried to roll away from him, but he stopped her by placing a hand in the middle of her stomach and pinning her flat to the mattress. "I'm taking a look at your feet one way or another. Which way do you prefer?"

Margo went limp and stared at the ceiling. "Hurry up and do it," she snapped.

When he didn't move, she glanced at him and caught him smiling. "You're a dirty old man, Ry. I'm talking about my feet."

Still smiling, he examined the soles of her feet, one at a time. When he was finally satisfied she hadn't been cut, he left her and retrieved a broom and began to clean up the broken shards of glass.

Slowly Margo pulled herself up and rested her back against the headboard. Still fuming, angry that he'd had the gall to chain her like an animal, she said, "So efficient. Do you make beds, too?"

He dumped the swept-up glass in the trash. "I live alone, remember? If I want my bed made more than once a week, I have to make it."

Margo sniffed and rubbed her wrists. "So who was at the door? Anyone I know?"

"Yeah, you know her." He stuck the broom out into the hall and then returned to sit in the paisley chair.

Was it the woman who had called him yesterday? Is that who had come knocking? Margo refused to feel jealous. "Are you going to tell me who it was, or are we back to playing games?"

"Last night's game had a happy ending."

Margo glared at him. "Never again."

"Never say never, baby."

"If you're not going to tell me who was at the door, there's no sense being in the same room with you." She swung her leg over the side of the bed in an attempt to leave, but he reached out and laid a hand on her knee. Quietly he said, "Your mother."

"My mother. My mother!" Margo knocked his hand off her knee and leaped to her feet. "What was my mother doing here? Does she know I'm here?" She turned away, thinking. "No, of course she doesn't know I'm here. If she did I would be facing her at this very minute." She spun back, demanded, "What did she want? Tell me everything you said to her."

"She came to ask a favor."

"A favor? Of you? When hell freezes."

"It's true. She wanted me to see if I could find you. It seems she called your friend's apartment looking for you, and your lie fell apart. She's worried. I considered leading her upstairs to ease her mind, but—"

Margo ignored his teasing and began worrying her lip. She should never have made up that story. It hadn't been a fail-safe lie like Blu had taught her.

"You never told me your mother liked me."

Margo watched him stand and strip off his shirt and toss it in the direction of the hamper near the closet door. "My mother doesn't like you."

"Sure she does. She told me so."

"As usual, your ego could use scissors." Margo sank into the stuffed chair Ry had just vacated, then bolted back up, too anxious to stay put. "So what did you tell her?"

He disappeared into the closet and returned wearing a white T-shirt stretched over his broad shoulders. He found a spot by the door and leaned against the wall, one hand resting on his hip. "I told her as soon as I found you, I would have you call her. We'll wait an hour and then you can phone her. Tony told her you were sick. Now she doesn't know what to believe."

"So I'm expected to tell another lie or get sick?"

"She went by your apartment. We're just lucky she didn't go inside. When you didn't answer the door she left."

This situation just kept souring in all directions. Margo couldn't wait to hear more *good* news.

"She tried to find Blu," he offered.

"With no luck," Margo finished. "I suppose Brodie was next on her list."

"You guessed it. It looks like you'll have to tell another tall tale, or be prepared to confess everything. Which I don't think would be a bad idea. Your mother's no dummy. And she's tougher than you think."

"I can't tell her Blu's disappeared. Brodie, too. There's nothing positive I can say right now to give her any hope. I hate lying," Margo sighed. "It always makes things worse."

"I hate lying, too."

His words were softly spoken, half strength, but they riled her just the same. "But you do it so well, Detective Archard. You certainly had me going a few hours ago. It brings back memories of another time and place, don't you think?" The sarcasm hid her hurt. Thankfully. Margo watched him narrow his eyes and shove away from the wall.

"You're no slouch yourself, baby. How many lies have you told in the past three days?"

His question gave her pause. Yes, she'd told a dozen-plus lies. Were those lies any more justified than Ry's? She didn't know, but she didn't intend to apologize for any of them.

"Let's not fight, baby. It won't help."

His rich voice was soothing. Angry about that, angry that she still couldn't hate *everything* about him, Margo snapped, "And what will help, Ry? You told me to lie to Mama. It's your fault I'm faced with telling her another one now."

"No. You said you couldn't tell her the truth. I simply insisted you return the phone message she left on your answering machine."

"What was I supposed to say? Sorry I missed your call, Mama. Oh, by the way, I was shot last night, my apartment has been trashed, Blu and Brodie are missing, and Ryland Archard has me under house arrest in his bedroom."

"When you put it that way, I vote for another lie."

Margo flopped down in the chair and buried her head in her hands.

"I know this is hard, baby, but until we find out who's after Blu, we're going to have to work together on this."

His voice was close. Margo looked up to find him kneeling beside her. Right now she needed a pair of strong arms to curl into, but she didn't dare allow herself the weakness. She needed to stay angry. She needed to remember what Ry was capable of. She jumped up and put some distance between them. "We may have to work together, but that's all we're doing together, Ry. Understand?"

Suddenly Margo's stomach growled.

"You're hungry. You probably haven't eaten all day."

No, she hadn't, but who could think of food at a time like this? "I don't want anything to eat."

He shoved to his feet. "You've got to eat. Lets go downstairs, and I'll see what I can find. Afterward you can call your mother."

Margo watched him stretch, yawn, then yawn again, and that's when the most fabulous idea slipped quietly into her subconscious. She said, "You go ahead. I'll be right down."

"If you're not, I'll be back up to get you," he warned.

"You won't have to. I'll be down," Margo promised. "And I'll cook. It might help me relax."

Margo watched Ry lean against the door and yawn for the tenth time since they left the kitchen table. They were back upstairs, in the bedroom again, his mood as sour as she'd ever seen it. Her mood, however, was the best she'd experienced in days—freedom was just minutes away.

"Hurry up, get your clothes off," he ordered as he shed his T-shirt and tossed it in the chair. Another yawn. He turned to see that she hadn't moved to do as he'd asked. "I said, get undressed. What are you waiting for?"

For you to fall over, Margo wanted to say. Instead she said, "I won't sleep in the same bed with you."

"You did last night. You even liked it."

"That was before I was reminded how much I hate you."

He blinked his eyes trying hard to stay awake. "I'm not going to force myself on you. I don't think I could tonight if I wanted to. What I need right now is sleep."

"Go sleep in the hammock."

"Last time I did that I got a sore neck." He unsnapped his jeans in a lethargic motion, then fumbled to find his zipper.

All she had to do was stall a little while longer, five minutes, max.

He sat on the edge of the bed and pulled off his boots. When he stood, he wobbled slightly.

Margo's confidence soared, then it was suddenly doused when he pulled his handcuffs from his back pocket. "What are you going to do with those?"

He turned to look at her. "What do you think?"

Margo shook her head. "You can't, Ry! You wouldn't!"

He stepped out of his jeans and briefs at the same time and stood beautifully naked holding the handcuffs loosely in his hand. His eyes were half-closed, his chest impossibly hard, and his long legs looked like sturdy oak trees—solid and unwavering. He was semiaroused, and he appeared more alert than he'd been for the past half hour. Clearheaded and perfectly rational.

That was impossible.

"Get your clothes off, baby, or I'll do it for you."

Margo swore silently and reached for the top button on her shirt. Making more work out of it than necessary, she slowly undid one button at a time.

"Need some help?" he warned.

"I don't have a bra on," Margo protested.

"And that means what?"

She called him a dirty name, then finished unbuttoning her shirt. She eased it off her injured shoulder first before shrugging out of it the rest of the way. She watched his gaze settle on her bare breasts.

He must have the constitution of an ox, Margo thought.

She let her shirt fall to the floor, then slowly slipped out of her jeans, keeping her panties on. As she straightened, he reached for her good arm, clamped one of the cuffs around her wrist, then snapped the other cuff around his own.

This wasn't part of the plan, Margo wanted to scream, but instead she was forced to deal with the heat from Ry's naked body. She tried to control her response, tried to gain as much distance as the cuffs would allow. Using anger to keep her grounded, she rattled the cuff clamped around her wrist. "I can't sleep like this, Ry. Take it off. Please!"

He stared at her for a long minute, then shook his head. "This is insurance, baby. When I open my eyes in the morning the first thing I want to see is you lying next to me." He tugged her toward the bed, tossed back the covers, then dragged her along with him as he literally fell into bed.

Sleep snared him a minute later.

Brodie Hewitt had a steel jaw. Any normal man would have passed out hours ago, Taber determined, watching the man take another bone-crushing blow.

They had been chipping away at duFray's foreman since Taber had taken him off the *Nightwing* at gunpoint. He hadn't expected Hewitt's muscle to be backed by brains, or that the bastard would be so damn quick. He'd been confident that his own man could easily handle a poorly educated fisherman. But he'd been wrong. From the very moment Antos had faced off with Hewitt, Taber had known they were in trouble.

Realizing his error, Taber had removed himself from the path of danger and pulled his .25-caliber Beretta from his jacket pocket. Unfortunately, his aim had been off a good couple of inches when he'd pulled the trigger, and the bullet nearly took Antos's head clean off.

The incident was not only unfortunate, but messy. At gunpoint, he'd ordered Hewitt to toss Antos's body overboard, then he'd forced the burly fisherman off the boat and into the trunk of his car.

"What is it now?" Taber shoved away from the wall he'd been leaning against and motioned to his two idiot cousins as they entered the warehouse. He couldn't stand the one called Raynard, but Rudy, not much better, had at least an ounce of brains and didn't sweat all the time. "Have you found her? Did she turn up at the Toucan?"

"No, we haven't found her yet," Rudy answered back.

"Maybe she's run off," Raynard suggested.

The obvious got Raynard a slap alongside the head from his brother. "We got a few more places to check out, boss. She'll turn up. We'll just keep looking till we find her."

"She's probably scared."

Stating another obvious fact got Raynard another

slap. "Of course she's scared," Rudy said. "You shot her."

"I didn't mean to. Maybe she drowned. I've been thinkin'—"

"Don't," Taber snapped, "just do as you're told." He turned away from the idiots, refusing to believe that Margo duFray's life had ended in the river. He also refused to believe these two men were truly related to him.

He focused on the former, something he actually could do something about. He'd been thinking about "Beautiful" for two days now, even when his thoughts should have been solely on the recovery of his stolen merchandise. He'd gone so far as to envision her in his penthouse, all that black hair spread across his white carpet. She'd be naked of course, her arms outstretched, begging him to join her.

His men had tied Brodie Hewitt to a wooden support in his warehouse, a support twice the man's size to ensure there would be no more surprises. "Did you hear that, Hewitt? They think she's dead. Is she?" Taber pulled the blue chemise from his pocket and waved it in front of the man's battered face. "She's not at her apartment, we checked."

On seeing the silk chemise in Taber's hand, Brodie Hewitt went crazy. He snarled like a dog and fought the ropes like a wild bull. But in the end, defeated, he sagged against the wooden support.

"I admire loyalty," Taber said smoothly. "Yours, however, boarders on stupidity. I could kill you right now." He eyed the blood trailing past Brodie's cheek, then smiled. "But I don't think you've suffered enough to have it end so quickly. Not near enough. Make him bleed, boys. And this time, I want to hear him scream."

As his men went back at Brodie Hewitt, Taber glanced over his shoulder to find that his two cousins were still there, hands in their pockets, looking ridiculous. "What are you standing around for? Do I have to draw you two a damn picture? I want things the way they were three days ago. I want my merchandise, and I want the woman. Do you understand?"

"You didn't have the woman three days ago," Raynard pointed out.

Rudy hit his brother again, then grabbed him by the collar and pulled him toward the warehouse door before Taber decided to kill another one of his men. The one no one would miss.

Chapter 10

Ry woke to the sound of music. Only, the music coaxing him awake wasn't the kind of music he normally listened to. It sounded more like something Jackson would like, fast paced and too loud.

He blinked open his eyes and found he was in his own bed. That much was reassuring, but the splitting headache driving nails through his skull was not. He tried to move his arm, tried to sit up. The sound of metal rattling sent another sharp pain shooting through his head. Again he wrestled with himself to sit up, which was impossible.

"What the hell…" He angled his head, saw his wrist chained to the bed.

"Need some help, partner?"

Ry jerked his head toward the window and found Jackson leaning against the wall watching what was left of the day go by. "How long have I been out?" he managed, still muzzy headed.

"All day. Must have been one helluva mickey."

"Shut up, Jackson, and cut me loose!"

Jackson turned from the window. "Take it easy. I haven't been sleepin' the day away like you. I've got a tail on her, so rest easy."

"She's gone?"

"Took flight sometime in the middle of the night is my best guess."

"But you know where she is, right?"

"I do." Jackson strolled forward, motioning to Ry's wrist and the set of cuffs that shackled him to the bedpost. "Damn inventive, Margo duFray. Gutsy, too. I do like a woman who knows how to take charge."

Ry jerked on the cuffs. "Get my key, dammit."

"I hope you can at least remember the good parts." Jackson bent and picked up Ry's jeans from the floor beside the bed. After going through the pockets and coming up empty, he reached into his own pocket and produced his set of keys.

"She must have drugged me," Ry reasoned. "I feel like hell."

"You look like it, too."

"Cut me loose," Ry demanded.

Jackson unlocked Ry's cuffs and freed his partner from the bedpost. "I looked around. Found an empty bottle of sleeping pills in the medicine cabinet along with a mess of other stuff. What the hell's going on with you, partner? If I didn't know better I'd say you had a healthy sideline going."

Ry caught the look Jackson was giving him. The look said I'm waiting for an explanation. "I used to have trouble sleeping. I haven't used any of that stuff in over a year."

"There's more there than just simple sleeping pills. A complete pharmacy from A to Z."

"I used to go to a shrink. He had me on some antidepressants. A whole bunch of crap. I'm through with that."

"Then why do you still have it around?"

"So I don't forget how low a man can sink," Ry answered bitterly. He sat up, then slowly tried to stand. Dizzy, he swayed into Jackson's waiting arms. "You should have tried to wake me earlier," he grumbled.

"I did. Once at seven-thirty this morning when I got here, then again at nine. I gave up around two in the afternoon. She must have given you enough to knock an elephant to his knees. Maybe she was trying to kill you, you think?"

"Maybe," Ry agreed. He sure felt like a corpse. "If you know where she is, why isn't she back here?"

"I was going to pick her up. Then I thought maybe she could lead us to her brother."

"She doesn't know where he is," Ry growled, forcing himself to stand on his own two feet. "I want her back here, dammit!"

"Because she's part of the case? Or is there something you neglected to mention?"

Ry swore. "It wouldn't have changed anything even if you had known Margo and I have a past. I'm not willing to put her life in jeopardy again, Jackson, and that's the bottom line."

"Again."

"Yes, dammit, again. And no, I don't want to explain."

The tone in his voice clearly let Jackson know there would be no further discussion on the subject.

"While you were sleeping, I called the precinct and talked to Andy. The report came in on yesterday's floater."

"And?"

"And Anthony Taos works for Denoux Inc., that import-export outfit on the waterfront. Andy says the blood on the deck of the *Nightwing* is a perfect match to Taos. Cause of death, head wound at close range. Probably a .25 caliber. Andy said you were right. The floater was in the water twelve hours max. Those damn crabs can raise a lot of hell once they find a meal that ain't going nowhere. The man's nose and fingers were still intact."

"Who do you have tailing Margo?"

"Frankie Costanini. Until I relieve him, he knows he's her shadow."

"And what has she been doing since she left here?"

"I can't tell you where she was before eight-thirty this morning, but I can detail every hour after that. I ran her down at…" Jackson pulled out a notepad. "At 8:36. She was at her mother's place. She spent three hours there, then at 11:20 she headed to the Toucan Lounge. She talked with Tony Bichon and a waitress named Angie Carson." He paused to read his stingy handwriting. "She returned to her apartment at 1:10 and made a phone call to Brodie Hewitt around 1:30. Tapping her apartment phone was a good idea, but it didn't get us anything. Hewitt didn't pick up. Frankie's been watching her place ever since. She's been cleaning up her apartment."

In the bathroom Ry pulled himself slowly together. He felt like hell, but more than that, he felt like a damn idiot. He should have expected something like this. Margo had never been the type to sit back and do nothing.

You would have thought he was a damn amateur the way he had let her con him. Maybe Clide was right, maybe he had no business working on a case that he was emotionally involved in.

Ry stared at himself in the mirror. Margo had drugged him, for God's sake, with his own sleeping pills no less. He should have thought something was fishy when she had insisted on cooking supper for him. But then he'd been too damn busy trying to smooth her ruffled feathers to analyze her sudden interest in raw hamburger patties.

After she'd done the dirty deed, he still hadn't caught on, not even after he couldn't stop yawning and his eyes had felt like they weighed a hundred pounds apiece.

He was willing to admit she'd outsmarted him and that his pride had been stung in the process. One part of him wanted to strangle her, but the other part applauded her determination.

Ry braced his hands on the sink and closed his eyes. Suddenly, out of nowhere a hazy image surfaced—an image of a warm body straddling him, a pair of hands touching him. Then he heard a voice, Margo's voice next to his ear.

He squeezed his eyes tight, concentrated on remembering. What had she whispered? What had she felt she could say to him asleep that she couldn't say to him awake? He had to know.

A half hour later, showered and shaved, Ry entered the kitchen to find Jackson in front of the stove cooking him a mess of eggs. When his partner glanced up, he said, "I thought some food in your belly might bring you around quicker. It's suppertime, anyway."

"I'm in a hurry," Ry insisted, glancing at his watch. It was almost seven. What did Margo have planned for tonight? Would she go to work, or did she have plans to shake the tail Jackson had put on her and go looking for trouble?

"I just called Frankie. Margo's fine. Like I said, she's picking up the mess our friends left and carrying it out to the trash in the back alley. There's time, and we need to talk."

Ry was in the middle of pouring himself a cup of coffee. He glanced up, not ready to hear any more bad news, but by the tone in Jackson's voice, it wasn't good news. "What is it?"

Jackson stepped back from the stove. "I went looking for Goddard last night like you said. I couldn't find him. I talked to a few of the old birds in the square, but nobody's seen him."

Ry swore.

"I'm not saying he's dead," Jackson offered.

"You're not saying he's alive, either."

"He probably skipped with your hundred bucks."

"That's crap and you know it."

Jackson stepped forward and slid the eggs he'd fried onto a waiting plate and delivered the plate to the table as though he'd been a waitress all his life instead of a cop. Ry eyed the plate, the neat way the eggs were arranged, the way the silverware sat atop the folded napkin on the table. "You a short-order cook in another lifetime, Jackson?"

His partner moved back to the sink. "So I cook. My mother owns a restaurant and she advised me to learn. She said the chance of a woman putting up with me was slim to none. I guess she was right. The way things stand, I couldn't buy a date in this town if I owned the city and promised the little lady half."

A touch of a smile parted Ry's lips as he pulled out a chair and sat. "So you're looking for a wife, is that it?"

Jackson poured himself a cup of coffee, then leaned against the counter. "Women don't naturally fall for cops, partner. Or haven't you noticed?"

Ry nodded, then took a bite of over-easy eggs. He knew all too well the risks a woman faced if she got involved with a cop.

"So what's next? You want me to go pick up Margo and bring her back here?" Jackson asked.

Ry sipped his coffee. "My first reaction would be yes. Drag her back here kicking and screaming if you have to."

"So you can lock her up again?"

"It would be for her own good," Ry reasoned.

Jackson nodded. "You're probably right, but what makes you think it'll work this time? It didn't before. Sooner or later—"

"It would work. I'd know what to expect."

"Maybe. Maybe if she pulled the same scam. A smart lady wouldn't."

Ry shoved the empty plate to the middle of the table. "Should I be off this case, Jackson? Is my judgment on this one way off?"

Jackson shrugged his wide football shoulders. "Truth?"

"Truth."

"If you have to ask me that, then maybe you should be. We haven't worked that long together, but from what I've seen, you usually don't sit back content to wait like this. If you hesitate, analyze the situation too long, you lose your edge. That's what you told me once. You also said it makes a cop vulnerable and puts the people around you in danger."

To hear his words tossed back at him was sobering, but it was also what he needed to hear. If he couldn't take charge of the situation, then he should let someone else take over.

"I'm surprised the chief didn't pull you off this case at the beginning, or doesn't he know about Margo?"

"Clide knows about Margo. But he didn't until yesterday."

"Withholding evidence." Jackson grinned. "And here I thought I was the only one who did things like that."

"So it's time to make a move, is that what you're saying?"

"That's about it. You want my angle on it?"

"Go ahead."

"I'd set up a sting. I'd let Margo out on a short leash and wait to see who came sniffing around."

"Use her as bait?" Ry nodded. "That's what she suggested last night."

Ry sat back and sucked down his coffee while his partner continued to amaze him by putting the kitchen back in order. It seemed Jackson was as comfortable with a fry pan and dishrag as he was with the Diamondback .38 he carried under his shirt.

He said, "I'm pretty sure Margo will head for the Toucan tonight, that is if I don't come after her. She's too loyal to Tony to miss another night behind the piano."

"The Toucan's crowded on Saturday nights," Jackson reminded. "That could be good or bad, depending on which way you look at it."

"Let's hope good." Ry checked his watch, then stood. "She goes onstage in a little over an hour. That doesn't give us much time to set it up."

Jackson pulled the towel he'd been using as an apron from his belt and hung it beneath the sink. "So do I replace Frankie? I'm still on suspension."

"That's never stopped you from getting involved before. Besides, Frankie has no experience with a woman like Margo. She's smarter than most."

Jackson paused at the door. Grinning over his shoulder, he said, "She must be. She made a fool out of you. And that, partner, ain't easy to do."

She'd been tailed all day by a hairy youth who chained smoked like a veteran and paced with a nervous skip that drew more attention than if he'd tied balloons on his ears. Moments ago the clown had been replaced by old reliable. But Jackson Ward, unlike the youth, looked neither nervous nor tormented by an annoying habit he couldn't control. For the past half hour he'd been leaning against the building across the street, and for the past five minutes he'd been cleaning his fingernails with a knife that was better suited to gutting a deer.

So where was Ry? Margo wondered. Was he still sleeping? She had expected to see him early afternoon. And when he hadn't showed, she'd decided

surely by suppertime. Only now it was past seven
and frankly she was getting worried. She didn't want
to worry about a man she should hate, but there it
was. Maybe he shouldn't have eaten that third hamburger. Maybe…

No, Ry had been breathing fine when she'd left
him. More than fine, actually. She wasn't going to
let her imagination run wild.

Pushing Ry from her thoughts, Margo glanced
around her ruined apartment. She'd spent most of
the day cleaning, piling the rubble into boxes and
hauling it to the trash. It would take several days to
make it look like anything, but it hadn't looked that
great to begin with, so she wasn't going to lose any
sleep over the end result. If she didn't have any furniture for a while, she'd make do and sit on the
floor.

She checked the clock in the kitchen, the only one
in the apartment that still worked. It was seven-thirty
and that meant she had to get to work. That is, if
Jackson was going to allow her to walk past him on
her way to the Toucan. She was confident that he
would; otherwise she would already be back at Ry's
home.

She hoped so, anyway. She'd tried to be very visible today. If the men who trashed her place had
staked out her apartment, they certainly should have
spotted her by now. Yes, she was nervous, and more
than a little afraid using herself as bait, but there
didn't seem to be any choice. Too many days had
gone by without Blu contacting her.

She'd realized last night that in order to keep her
mother safe and do the best she could for Blu and
Brodie, she must tell her mother everything. Well,

maybe not everything, but at least about Blu and the situation at present. Actually it hadn't gone all that badly. And when it was over, she'd called Uncle Pike and had asked him to camp out on her mother's couch for a few days.

It had been hard to admit she'd lied, but her mother had surprised her with a huge hug, then the assurance that everything would work out, especially since Ryland Archard was on the case.

Ry was right. Mama did like him.

Margo stepped onto the sidewalk and forced herself to cross the street. She walked directly past Jackson, her heart pounding wildly as she tried not to look at him. To her relief he didn't try to stop her. She'd gone a block when she decided to look over her shoulder—Jackson had pocketed his knife and was now following her.

She reached the Toucan ten minutes later. She hadn't realized how hot it was outside until she stepped through the back door and cool air touched her flushed face. Two more steps and she tilted her head to catch the rich scent of blackened catfish— Tony's Saturday-night special. She'd only been gone a few days but she welcomed the familiar, knowing that tonight she would be appreciated and greeted warmly.

She walked up the short hall and peered into the lounge, not surprised to see the dining room crammed with wall-to-wall people. She made eye contact with Tony to let him know that she'd shown up like she promised. He nodded from behind the bar, then a smile took in his entire face.

"She's well," Tony shouted, kissing his fingers

and sending the gesture through the air to where Margo stood. "*Mais, yeah,* tonight we celebrate."

Margo laughed, then blew a kiss back to him. As she turned to go to her dressing room she glanced deeper into the dining room. She wasn't prepared to see Ry seated at his usual table, and the sight of him froze her on the spot. Immediately her insides tightened and her heart began to race.

Like magnets, their eyes met and held. Then Ry did something completely out of the ordinary—he saluted her with the beer that sat in front of him.

Never before had he acknowledged her in public. And as friendly as the gesture looked, Margo knew he must be furious with her for drugging him. She gauged the intensity of his blue eyes, and a chill crept up her spine. He looked more formidable and determined than ever. More handsome, too. On both accounts she was going to have to be on her guard.

Margo's breath left her lungs in a sudden whoosh. Thankful for the distance that separated them, she raised her chin. She had to be onstage in one hour, and she needed to get dressed, needed to concentrate on doing her best behind the piano. Even though that was the farthest thing from her mind, she needed to become the singer Chili duFray for a few hours.

She broke eye contact with Ry and headed for her dressing room. Inside, taking several calming breaths, she opened the closet where she kept a number of satin shirts and several pairs of tight jeans in various colors.

She'd been brought up a simple girl, and in most things her tastes reflected her upbringing. Still, when it came to entertaining in a city such as New Orleans, the exotic atmosphere required a complementary counterpart. In the past year, Margo had found a blend of her two worlds by wearing glamorous satin shirts and tight jeans. The combination was effective, especially when she accented the fashion statement with break-your-ankle spiked heels and an extra fifteen minutes in front of the mirror.

She stepped into a pair of skin-tight black jeans, then slipped on a loose chemise. She covered the chemise with a white, long-sleeved satin shirt that fell past her hips to graze her slender thighs. In front of the mirror, she checked in to make sure no one would be able to see the white bandage beneath the full sleeve of her shirt. Satisfied, she guided her feet into a pair of gold, three-inch, strappy spikes. Gold hoop earrings added a seductive flavor to her costume, as did a wide gold necklace, several gold bracelets, and last, an overstated imitation sapphire ring.

Her silky thick straight hair was easy, and she grabbed the brush on the vanity and skillfully brushed through the thickness, then added a sprinkle of diamond dust throughout and a pinky-finger amount to the corner of each dark eye. Last, she applied a spicy-flavored red lip gloss to her full lips. The look complete, she left her dressing room and headed for the small lit stage.

As she neared the lounge, she could hear Tony's flattering introduction. Then, without delay, she appeared before them and slipped behind the piano. The applause lasted through the introduction of her first song, a soft ballad she knew so well she could sing it in her sleep. Her job was not to distract the Toucan's customers, but to enhance the overall exotic atmosphere. Only Chili duFray, her sultry voice making love to each word she sang, easily captivated the customers and, like it or not, had become the main attraction from the first day she'd slipped behind the piano.

She moved into the next song, and the crowd reminded her with another round of applause just how much they had missed her. Forty-five minutes later Margo had succeeded in captivating her fans once more and was ready for her first break of the evening.

She had done well to ignore the corner where Ry sat, but as the dance crowd swelled, she chanced a discreet glance into the crowd and singled out the private table in the back of the room. She wasn't surprised to see a petite blonde in a pink dress covered by a zillion sequins sitting in the vacant chair next to Ry. It was no secret that Charmaine Stewart had been literally tripping over her own feet to get Ry to notice her for months.

Margo watched the pretty blonde laugh, smile like an electric eel, then lean forward to whisper something in Ry's ear. Like her father, Judge Stewart, Charmaine had made quite a name for herself in the society pages. The rumor mill lately hinted that the Judge's daughter was looking for a husband. Closer to the truth, Margo figured, it was the judge who was looking for a husband to keep his daughter out of the gossip columns. And what better man for the job than a sexy homicide detective who just happened to live in the Garden District.

Margo sniffed in disgust and turned back to her performance. One more song and she could escape back to her dressing room for some emotional fortification. Anxious to get offstage, she hastily picked a crowd favorite. She started the intro, the crowd applauded. Too late she realized her mistake; the sexy Toni Braxton song, "There's No Me without You," brought back a flood of memories.

While Margo suffered through the lyrics, Charmaine Stewart coaxed Ry onto the dance floor and snuggled close to his chest. Margo knew what it felt like to be in those powerful arms, could almost feel the heat, the hardness of his chest. To be on the receiving end of *that look,* the one he was so unaware of offering at the exact moment when—

Suddenly a flood of regret washed over Margo. She'd willingly fed her addiction, labeling it "just sex." But now Ry was haunting her thoughts like a demon, and the demon wouldn't let her forget the intense heat, the passion. The perfection.

His scent still lingered in her memory, and Margo swore, still on her skin. His voice could make her ache as easily as his touch. The painful truth was, Ry had always known how to handle her from the very beginning—where to touch her and what to say to make her visibly shudder. She had hoped, no prayed, she would outgrow him someday for sanity's sake, but two years later the feelings were just as intense. And the lovemaking…the lovemaking had gotten more intense, crazier and even hotter than she remembered.

The lyrics faded on Margo's lips as the last chord fell from her fingertips. She stood automatically, then headed offstage, the applause following her as she hurried to her dressing room.

Margo had a forty-minute break, and Ry intended to monopolize at least half of the time before she went back onstage. She may not be willing to give him the time, but he intended to take it anyway. And not privately in her dressing room, but out in the open.

Jackson was right. He'd been treading too easy when it came to the case, and the same applied when it came to Margo. And tonight Ry meant to change that—there would be no more sitting on the fence.

It would be something new for both of them—speaking to each other in public. He had been careful not to let on to anyone he and Margo shared a past, and in a city the size of New Orleans, that hadn't been too hard to accomplish. He was sure that's what had ensured Margo's safety two years ago in the Koch Menaro case. But as Clide had pointed out, Koch was dead—there was no reason why he and Margo couldn't speak, or more, in public if they wished. After all, his self-imposed rules had already been shot to hell. And honestly it felt good to be living again. Really living.

He ordered another beer, then leaned back in his chair. Again an elusive image from last night teased his senses, and for the umpteenth time since he'd opened his eyes and found himself handcuffed to his bedpost, Ry felt like a damn voyeur—waiting hungrily for some clue as to what had passed between him and Margo before she'd fled into the night. He knew something sure as hell had happened.

He checked his watch again. She'd been gone a long ten minutes. He decided he would give her another ten before he… She strolled back into the lounge wearing a false smile; Ry could tell it was forced by the tilt of her head and her rigid body language. She nodded to the men at the bar who were vocal enough to catch her attention. As she passed a table with a lone customer seated with his back to Ry, she stopped and spoke briefly. Ry craned his neck, saw the gentleman motion to the empty chair at his table. Relieved when Margo declined the offer, he discreetly signaled Jackson to check out the man at the table. Just as discreetly, Jackson agreed that the man was worth the effort.

As Margo drew closer, Ry could see her injured arm drawn close to her body. It must be hurting, he decided, with all the piano playing required of her tonight. He admired her loyalty and dedication, loved her regal appearance, even though it was nothing she needed to work very hard at. Her beauty was as natural and breathtaking as a coastal sunrise.

"So," she stopped and placed her hand on the back of the vacant chair next to him, "sleep all day or did you make it up for lunch? I left extra hamburger in the fridge."

Her smile suddenly turned real, as well as smug. It clearly told Ry, she felt justified in drugging him. Still, he hadn't expected her to rub his nose in it with so much obvious pleasure.

As she pulled out the chair and sat, he glanced around and noticed that the crowded tables around them had turned quiet. Knowing there was a good chance they had an audience, he said, "That was nice of you to think ahead, the hamburger, I mean. Only you forgot to unchain me from the bed, baby. Fair is fair, but if you want me to keep playing your games, the least you could do in the morning is—"

Her hand shot out and covered his mouth. Embarrassed, she side-glanced the couple at the table next to them. Ry watched her cheeks turn a warm glowing shade of pink. She said to the couple, "He's always joking around. Really, we never. I didn't—"

Amused, Ry waited for her to bring her attention back to him. And as he'd expected when they were face-to-face once more, her eyes flashed fire. Softly, but with a mountain of feeling, she said, "That was cruel."

"What was cruel was feeding me drugged hamburger," Ry answered just as quietly, but with the same intensity she had chastised him.

"You complained about being tired. I was just helping out by offering you an uninterrupted eight hours." Her smug smile returned. "Or fifteen. Exactly how long did you sleep?"

Ry studied her in silence.

She leaned forward. "Sulking doesn't suit you, Detective Archard."

"Gloating doesn't suit you, either."

"You can't be surprised." She glanced around, then lowered her husky voice once more. "Like you don't know why I did it. You lied to me about something critical. If you ever do it again, be prepared for more of what you got last night. I'm no child, Ry. No fool, either."

Ry sighed. "I needed you to be honest with me. You weren't doing that. I used poor judgment in a crunch situation, I admit that, but—"

"Is that how you're justifying inhuman behavior? Poor judgment?"

He swore softly. "Contrary to what you believe, I don't enjoy lying any more than you do." Ry tried to keep his voice in control, but every time he thought about the seriousness of the situation his temper flared.

"Just so you know, I told Mama about Blu this morning. Everything is out in the open. No more lies."

"And how did that go?"

"Well enough."

"So she took it like a trooper. Didn't I say she'd—"

"I also left strict instructions with Uncle Pike to stay with Mama until this is all over."

"That was smart."

She was all business. Feeling the need for some form of contact, Ry reached out and gripped her fingers. She tried to tug free, but he refused to let her go. "I forgive you for last night."

"Well, I don't forgive you."

She was back to being obstinate, and Ry knew it was fueled by the knowledge that she had reestablished her freedom, or so she thought. "How about a truce?"

"No."

"A deal, then?"

"No."

"I could have had you picked up hours ago," Ry told her. "Jackson spotted you on your way to see your mother this morning."

"No deal," she said again, then, as if she had just remembered something, she attempted to stand. Ry tightened his hold on her and forced her back into the chair. "You don't have to be back onstage for another fifteen minutes."

"Let go," she whispered hotly.

"Make a scene," Ry urged calmly. "I dare you."

"I don't want to make a scene, but I don't want to be sitting here when your date returns from powdering her nose, either. So let go."

Instead of doing as she asked, Ry threaded his fingers through hers like a puzzle piece that had found the perfect fit. "Are we talking about Char?"

"You know *we* are."

Ry studied Margo's face. Her eyes were almost black, and her breathing had gone deeper. If he didn't know better, he would think she was jealous. Liking the idea, he said, "She's not my date, baby. You don't have anything to worry about—"

"Me worry about you? You're joking of course."

"Tell me about last night."

"You know what happened last night."

She twisted her hand free, and Ry let her. He leaned forward. "I mean after you drugged me. Tell me what happened in that bed?"

He watched her sit back, take a couple of quick breaths. "You want to know how I got the key and left, fine. I waited until I was sure you were sleeping and…" She lowered her voice. "I managed to reach for your pants and took the key from the pocket."

"My pants were on the floor. You were handcuffed to me on the opposite side of the bed."

"It wasn't easy getting the key. I never said it was."

"You touched me."

A few more short breaths of air. "Of course I touched you. I had to crawl over you. Stop looking at me like that."

"Like what?"

"Like you know something."

"Something?"

"You couldn't possibly know..." She stopped herself. "You were asleep."

"Couldn't know what? That you touched me?" Ry hoped she would confess something, anything that might spark his memory. He needed to know what happened, what she'd said. "You whispered in my ear."

"Oh, God!" She stood quickly, nearly knocking over the chair in the process.

Ry reached out and snared her hand. "Your breathing's gone wild, baby." She sat back down.

"Stop this. You're causing another scene. I like my job. I like these people, and they like me. I don't want anything to ruin it. So just stop."

"Okay. I'll stop for now. We can discuss it later, back at the house."

"No."

"I was afraid you were going to be stubborn." Ry released her hand, leaned back and crossed his arms over his chest, the action stretching his navy-blue shirt taut over his broad shoulders. "If you don't come home with me be prepared to be arrested."

"Arrested? For what?"

With as fierce an expression as he could muster, Ry said, "Attempted murder."

She stared in disbelief. "Who did I try to murder?"

"Me. Last night."

She narrowed her beautiful brown eyes. "That's ridiculous."

Ry shrugged.

"You wouldn't do it."

"Wouldn't I? I've done worse, right?" He leaned

forward and whispered, "There's something else I should warn you about." Slowly he reached out, clasped her around the neck, and pulled her close. "I want you back in my life, in my bed." That said, Ry slanted his mouth over hers and kissed her. It was a kiss like in the old days, a kiss loaded with innuendo and more than one future promise. And by the time he had finished staking his claim on her, there was more than one table watching the performance offstage.

Lucky breaks didn't shine down on Margo often. Recently they had been as spare as Ry's presence in her life. So when the fight broke out at the bar, she saw it as the perfect diversion for the perfect escape.

Seated behind the piano, finishing the final chorus of her last song of the evening, Margo watched Ry leap to his feet and head to the bar where Charmaine Stewart had become the elusive prize in a tug-of-war between two oversize admirers. As she was nearly being torn into two lovely sequined pieces, she continued to scream at the top of her lungs, crying out for Ry to help her.

Margo ignored her irritation at hearing Ry's name on Charmaine Stewart's lips and instead concentrated on getting offstage as quickly as possible. With every eye turned toward the bar, she scrambled up from the piano bench and fled into the back hall. She didn't take time to think her plan through, all she knew was that she had to get away and quickly. Ry's heat-filled kiss had her questioning too many things. True, the damn thing had had enough punch and dynamite behind it to knock her into next week, but what about the past? And what did he mean, he wanted her back in his life?

It was all some kind of trick, she decided. A mean, calculated device to pay her back for drugging his supper and chaining him to the bedpost.

As she reached her dressing room door, Margo glanced down at her three-inch spikes, then over her shoulder. Afraid to take the time to change shoes, she sighed and hurried past her dressing room. Taking another quick look behind her, she flung the back door open and ran straight into the arms of one of the Toucan's customers.

"Oh!" Margo jumped back and promptly stumbled. But before she fell, the man's hand shot out to rescue her. She felt his firm grasp clamp down on her injured arm as he hauled her upright, felt the stitches draw. She moaned in response, then made the situation worse by tugging her arm free. "Excuse me, I...I wasn't watching where I was going and—"

"Then you weren't throwing yourself into my arms? What a pity," the man said smoothly. "I had hoped that was the case."

The easy smile that he flashed her was friendly enough, and yes, he was handsome in an eccentric sort of way, but Margo didn't smile back. She took in the man's clothing, noting he was dressed all in black, his long hair falling well past his shoulders. He reminded her of a swashbuckling pirate. The only thing missing was one of those nasty-looking guns shoved into his belt and a black eye patch.

"I'm in a hurry," Margo said, then emphasized the fact by glancing behind her. She was relieved when the hall remained empty.

"Don't tell me that hell's devils are chasing you?" he teased.

"No." Margo shook her head.

"Then you don't need to be rescued, is that it, *Beautiful?* It's raining, and my car is right outside."

Margo hesitated. A quick escape would be the best. Even if Ry wasn't on her heels, he could be at any second. "Yes, I think..." In midsentence, she stopped herself. If she got into this man's car, her chance of flushing out Blu's enemy might be taken away. At this very moment someone might be watching her, waiting for the opportunity to speak to her. It was a frightening thought, but also the only chance she had of finding Blu.

"Thank you for being a gentleman, but I'll confront the rain and hell's devils if I need to," Margo told the pirate, then moved past him quickly and hurried into the alley.

The rain had turned the sultry air sticky, and the smells from the city rose up to greet her as she reached the street. The rain quickly soaked her shirt, and it clung to her curves like a second skin. Wiping the rain from her eyes, Margo suddenly wished she'd taken the stranger up on his offer. She glanced back to see if she could find him. When she saw no one, she considered her options and decided her apartment was the closest place to go.

Minutes later, soaked to the bone and breathless, Margo entered her apartment building. She hurried up the steps and down the hall. Chest heaving, she sagged against the dingy wall next to her front door and forced air back into her lungs. Eyes closed, she tried to slow her pounding heart.

A sudden noise warned her of impending danger. Margo jerked away from the wall, but it was too late. Her apartment door swung open and a hand shot out from the darkness and pulled her inside.

Chapter 11

"I'm getting too old for this crap. I haven't run four blocks flat-out since I made detective."

"Ry! I thought—"

"Jackson's taking care of Char Stewart."

He had her pinned, her chest flattened against the door, his body pressed into her back. He was breathing heavily, his moist breath moving in and out against her ear. The room had suffered from the day's high humidity, and in the darkness Margo could feel the sultry heat, hear her own heavy breathing. She said, "Back off, Ry."

"Why, am I hurting you?"

"No—yes."

"Which is it, baby?"

"Yes!"

"I don't think so." He sighed, then leaned his head against the door beside hers. "I'm tired of running after you, tired of hiding how I feel, tired of keeping my hands off you.''

"Ry, please back off." Margo attempted to turn around, but he pressed his weight more firmly against her. "Ry...Ry, please—"

She felt his hand on her hip, slowly it slid down her thigh. "Say no," he murmured. "See if it will make a difference."

He pressed his fingers into her thigh and slowly dragged them back up. Margo would have been afraid, if the man behind her was someone else. But this was Ry Archard, the man with the golden touch and drug-filled kisses. And though his tone suggested he was angry, that his temper had been stretched, she knew he wouldn't hurt her.

She felt him shudder, felt her own body tremble. Margo bit her lip and squeezed her eyes shut. She couldn't stop thinking about his mouth on hers, couldn't stop thinking about what it would be like to have him make love to her right here, right now.

"Halfway through your last set, I remembered," he whispered against her ear.

"Remembered?"

"What happened last night."

Margo sucked in her breath, squeezed her eyes tight. "You were asleep," she insisted. "You couldn't know."

His hands proved her wrong. Suddenly he was pulling her away from the wall just enough to touch her breasts in the same manner she had touched his chest last night. The action forced her backside into his groin and Margo sucked in her breath. "I'm still angry with you for running away from me," he told her, "but—"

"You're mistaken if you think I care," she argued.

"We'll see what you care about," he breathed against her ear. His hands clasped her wrists and he lifted her arms and placed them, palms flat, against the door. A moment later, he nudged her legs apart. His hands returned to her waist.

"Ry, please!"

"Please, what, baby?" He gyrated his hips against her perfectly shaped butt, letting her know how advanced his condition was. He dipped his head, found her exposed neck, nipped and teased. His hands captured her breasts. Margo's reaction to his thumbs grazing their already-puckered tips through the wet satin was a faint no. Her protest was embarrassingly weak, the pleasure as his fingers stroked her nipples causing her to moan pitifully. Easily, he coaxed another shameful moan from her, than another and another.

Margo struggled to regain her pride, only instead of moaning, she found herself sucking in her breath and sighing Ry's name as his skilled fingers continued to reinvent the meaning of the word *pleasure.*

Working her zipper down, he wedged his hand into her panties, his long fingers dipping downward to find her in as much need as he obviously was. "I thought so," he whispered, nipping her ear.

He was ruthless in his intent, barely letting her catch her breath before he moved on to his next assault. With his free hand, he shoved her jeans to her knees. Margo pressed her forehead against the door, bit down on her bottom lip to keep from moaning again.

"You're mine, baby. Admit it."

Stubbornly Margo shook her head.

"Say it. Say it!"

"Yes," Margo gasped as his fingers slid inside her. "Yes, damn you!"

She heard his zipper open, felt his hot flesh surge forward, then he was pulling her to him and bending her forward a little at the same time. His heat, when he entered her, scalded her. Margo moaned out her pleasure, then pressed backward to take all of him inside her. She trembled, clung to the door, as she arched her back and angled her head to feel his hungry mouth on her neck.

It was intense and quick. Mind numbing and sinfully satisfying. A slice of heaven on earth.

Breathless, Margo felt his body relax against her, then leave her altogether. She sagged into the door, her jeans and panties still clinging to her knees. She could hear his hard breathing, hear him working to right his own damp clothes.

"I'm sorry, baby, I shouldn't have come at you like that." She felt his hands on her once again, only this time he was carefully working her jeans and panties back up her thighs. Slowly he turned her to face him in the dark.

Margo didn't say anything and when the silence went on, he said, "I didn't hurt you. If I did, I—"

Margo kissed him quiet. She didn't want him apologizing, and right now she didn't have any words for him. In the old days he had loved her in a dozen different ways, and honestly she had enjoyed them all.

"Say something." He kissed her back, this time as if she was a fragile flower.

Margo stared up at him in the darkness, wishing

she could see his handsome face. "You know I never minded that—"

"I came at you from all angles." He sighed, kissed her nose. "Don't run away from me anymore, baby. It scares the hell out of me when you take off like that." When Margo didn't answer, he pulled her close and squeezed tightly. "Say you won't run. I need to hear—"

"Ouch!" Margo gasped as a sharp pain ricocheted down her arm.

Ry instantly released her. "What? What is it?"

"It's nothing. I—"

Before she could finish, he reached for the light switch and the upended room was flooded with light. But neither gave a second look at the piles Margo had made in an effort to clean up the mess. They were both staring at the blood-stained satin that clung to her arm.

"What the hell! Did I do that?" Ry demanded. "How? When?"

Margo studied the red stain, recalled when it must have happened. "You didn't do it, Ry. I did it," she insisted. "I almost took a spill out the back door at the Toucan, and—"

"Why didn't you say something? Here, let me see." Quickly he unbuttoned her shirt as if it were the most natural thing to do. Carefully, he slid the damp satin off her shoulders, then removed the blood-stained bandage. "The stitches look intact, but until I clean it up I won't know for sure."

Margo looked down to see his hands were shaking where they touched her arm. She glanced up to study the serious expression on his face. "It'll be fine. It doesn't hurt that bad."

"You've got to be more careful, dammit."

It was as if he wasn't listening. Margo frowned, thought she'd heard his voice tremble. "Ry…"

"I'll clean it first, then—"

"Ry?"

"Don't worry, baby. I'll take care of it, and—"

"Ry!"

He looked at her.

"Tell me," Margo reached out and took hold of his hand, "why you're shaking?"

He pulled his hand away. "It's nothing."

"I want to know why you're so upset. It's not like you. At least not like the old you."

"Later. Right now your arm needs—"

Margo pushed him away. "The deal is, you can repair the damage done to my arm if I get some straight answers to a few questions."

"Margo, this is serious." He motioned to her arm. "You're bleeding."

"A little blood is not going to kill me or I'd be already dead."

"Don't talk like that!"

"See. You get so upset about the silliest things."

"You're going to have a nasty scar. That's not silly, that's a damn shame. Senseless, really!"

Why was it every time she cracked a joke at her own expense Ry went ballistic? Again, Margo studied his face curiously. "I suppose letting you play doctor once more wouldn't hurt."

"No, it wouldn't."

"Then you agree?"

"Agree?"

"Say, yes, Margo, I accept your deal. I'll tell you anything you want to know. Just ask."

He was wearing a frown. Suddenly it slid to a half smile, and he leaned forward and kissed her. Then softly, his lips a mere inch from hers, he whispered, "Yes, baby, I accept the deal. That is, if I can play doctor as long as I want, in any way I choose."

"You're a dirty old man, Ry."

"You used to love the way I touched you, the way I had to have you the minute I knew you were burning."

Yes, she used to love his insistent hands and his visible need for her. She used to love his sexy body and his naughty blue eyes. The way he ate shrimp and wore those crazy Texas boots. Even the way that terrible cigarette dangled from his lips. The truth was, she used to love everything about Ry Archard and still did. In fact, she loved him more— the sensitive man who stood before her, for whatever reason, reminded her of a wounded hero.

She was a crazy fool, and he was going to hurt her again. But, yes, she loved him with an ache so huge she knew—no feared—that this time, when he walked out of her life, she would never be able to piece together her broken heart. Still, she couldn't stop loving him. Pretending to hate him was simply another lie she was tired of living with. She would love him until the day she died, and long after that. She just didn't have a choice in the matter.

Margo stepped away from the door, and as she walked past him, she reached out and snagged a couple of fingers on one of his big hands. "Come on, old man, let's see if we can find a clean washcloth in the bathroom."

They walked past the junk piles, then entered her

tiny bathroom. As Margo turned around, she found herself back in Ry's arms, his expression stone sober. "I'll find the bastards who shot you and ruined your place. Say you believe that, baby. Say you trust me, because you can, you know. You can trust me like no one else."

Normally she would have mocked his words to safeguard her own feelings, but he was so serious, and his words held such conviction. "I believe you'll find the creeps. Trusting you—" Margo shrugged "—that's going to be a little harder to come by." Then she surprised both of them and kissed him. It was light and quick, but sincere.

"What was that for?" he asked, his expression replete, yet curious.

Margo thought a minute, needed to say something. "For leaving Charmaine Stewart in your partner's capable hands, I guess."

"It was my pleasure."

"And mine," she agreed.

He glanced around her spare bathroom. The white walls were cracked and yellowed, the mirror over the narrow sink and been shattered, but it still hung intact. Margo could see that Ry was taking stock of her meager lifestyle with an unusual amount of interest. Yes, the place looked pathetic, and she felt a twinge of embarrassment over that. She could afford a better place if she wanted to, only that money had been better spent on keeping the fishing fleet alive. And as often as her brother had protested the money she'd offered him, Blu had swallowed his pride and taken it because they both had wanted the duFray Devils to survive.

"I'm not here much," she said when he faced her again. "Don't pity me, or the way I choose to live."

"I don't pity you." He touched her cheek. "I admire you. I always have. Sit down."

Margo perched on the toilet seat. She kept her mouth shut while he retrieved a clean washcloth from the cupboard and knelt in front of her. She watched as he concentrated on wiping the blood away. After a while he said, "Blu's lucky to have you as his sister. Do you suppose he realizes that?"

"Starting in on Blu isn't going to—"

"Stop defending him." He looked up, his blue eyes narrowed slightly. "He put you on DuBay Pier knowing it wasn't safe. For that I'm going to—"

Margo reached out and covered his mouth with her hand. "He didn't put me on the pier. It was my decision to leave the alley."

He kissed the palm of her hand, then returned it to her lap. "It was a dangerous decision."

"I'm not sorry."

"I've got mixed feelings about it." His hands stilled on her arm. "You could have been killed and that's not something I want to consider. But since you weren't... They say there's a reason why things happen the way they do. If you hadn't been shot and hadn't come to the house we might not have—"

"Slept together again?"

"You can't deny we're good together."

"I never denied it. Why did you walk away two years ago?"

She hadn't meant to ask him that. She'd always felt the excuse he'd offered back then, as paltry as it had been, was enough. How could *why* matter when the bottom line was he didn't want her any longer in his life?

"It's a long story." He busied himself with her arm again, tossed the blood-stained washcloth into the sink. "Two years ago my job got between us." He shook his head, began to bandage her arm. "I had resigned myself to accepting that. I'd worked out a way to live with it, and," he glanced up and smiled, "life wasn't great, but I was keeping it together." He finished binding her arm and sat back on his haunches. "Truth is, baby, I've been living a lie and I don't want to any longer."

He ran his fingers between her legs and parted them lightly. Coming up on his knees again, he moved between the notch he'd created. Slowly, his hands moved upward, over her thighs, past her trim waist to her breasts. His long fingers fanned out to feel all of her at one time, from seductive cleavage to the outer swell of each ripe mound. Margo closed her eyes and sucked in her breath. Then he was there, his mouth pressed against hers, sending her heart racing and her mind spinning.

When he had them both breathing hard, he backed off. "Open your eyes. I want you looking at me when I say this."

Eyes open, Margo locked gazes with him.

He drew in a long breath then let it out slowly. "Okay, here it is. I-I've never stopped loving you. That's the honest truth. I made you think otherwise, but that was the whole idea."

He attempted to kiss her again, but Margo arched back at the same time her hand went to his chest to keep him at bay. He couldn't love her and do what he'd done. It wasn't possible to hurt someone as badly as he'd hurt her and then say he'd loved her. Was he trying to trick her again? She dropped her hands back to her lap. "When you love someone, you don't destroy them, Ry. The day you left me, you said—"

"I said what I had to to keep you alive."

"That doesn't make sense."

He stood quickly. "I know it sounds crazy, but there was a good reason why I acted like a bastard. Why I said those things to you the day I walked out. I'll explain once we're home."

"Home? I never said I was going home with you."

"You can't stay here."

"I can if I want to."

"How badly do you want to learn the truth?"

Margo hesitated. She wanted more than anything to learn the truth, but—

"Maybe I was wrong," he said suddenly. "It might be easier if you never knew. If you just kept—"

Margo bristled. "I'm not a coward, Ry. If there's something I should know, then I want to hear it."

For a long minute they stared at each other, then he held out his hand, a smile finally parting his lips. "Then let's go home."

They drove through the Garden District in silence. Ry wasn't sure how he was going to explain two wasted years to Margo without her ending up hating him, but they had struck a deal, and now he was going to have to live up to his part of it.

Honestly, he hadn't planned on telling her about Koch Menaro until after he'd solved the Burelly case. He'd analyzed the situation while he'd sat and listened to her sing, and what he'd decided was that the best approach was the old approach. To win Margo back he would work her the way he had in the old days, slowly and inventively. Then, when he was sure she trusted him again, he would sit down with her one day, a few months from now, and come clean.

It was the coward's way, he knew that, but there was no easy way to tell the woman you loved that you had sacrificed their life together out of fear. But tonight that look in her eyes had changed his mind. She deserved to know the truth, every sordid detail. And in the end it would be her decision to forgive him or not.

It was still raining when Ry sped through the iron gate and up the incline into the carport. He shut the engine off, and they both sat there a minute. Finally he reached out and slid his arm around the back of Margo's seat. He moved in quickly, his intent obvious. She angled her head back against his arm and allowed him to kiss her. He did so carefully, moved his mouth over hers with gentle persuasion, then murmured, "Let's go inside."

Ry followed Margo into the kitchen moments later, flipping on the light as he closed the door behind him. He'd left the radio on as usual, and a soft sad song was playing. The coffeemaker was half-full. He watched her head for the coffee, watched her open the cupboard and reach for two yellow cups.

He'd gotten used to her in the kitchen over the past few days, even though it seemed strange. She fit it, but then she should, since he'd bought it with her in mind. He wondered what she'd say if she knew her name was on the deed.

"Why don't you go upstairs and get out of your wet clothes? Take a bath if you want, as long as you don't get your bandage wet, that is. I'll bring coffee," he promised.

She turned to look at him. "Are you always this helpful with your other houseguests?"

"I told you before, I don't have houseguests. What are you really asking, Margo? What is it you want to know?"

She raised her chin, gave that little spare sigh she always did when she was faced with a question she'd rather not answer. "It's not important."

"Ask it."

"All right. Has Charmaine Stewart ever been here?"

Ry didn't debate the question. He wasn't going to detail Char's visit, but he wasn't going to deny it, either. "Once."

"Once?"

"She arrived uninvited and didn't stayed long. We've never slept together if that's what your next question was going to be." He wouldn't go into the night Char had snuck up on him in the middle of the night while he was having one of his dreams about Margo. That would be too revealing right now, and he didn't want to feel any more vulnerable than he already did. Before the night was over Margo could very easily walk out of his life forever. If that happened he would need at least his pride left intact.

"I'll be upstairs," she said softly. "No hurry with

the coffee. I've decided the bath will do me some good.''

An hour later Ry was standing at the bedroom window when Margo stepped through the open door. It had stopped raining and the sky was clear, the moon out. He heard her whisper-soft steps, caught her seductive scent and turned slowly. She was wearing one of his shirts, her shapely legs and bare feet giving his heart a jolt.

She glanced at the unmade bed. ''You're slipping, Ry. I thought you said you made beds.''

''I do, but not with a headache and you on my mind. I woke up with both.''

She lowered her gaze to stare at the floor. ''I didn't try to kill you.''

''I know.''

She looked up. ''You shouldn't have eaten that third hamburger. I shouldn't have let you.''

''But they were so good,'' he teased hoping to lighten her spirits. He strolled to the nightstand, poured her a cup of coffee and offered it to her.

She accepted it, then asked, ''Why do you have all those pills in the medicine cabinet?''

With her simple question, Ry realized that the time had come. He could no longer avoid telling her about Koch Menaro and what had followed. ''Sit down, Margo.'' He pointed to the paisley chair and, once she was seated, he walked back to the window. ''We were together about a month. If you remember, that last week, I—''

''Started acting different.''

''I can still hear you saying, 'Are you crazy in love, or what?' You said it just like that.''

''I remember.''

"You were right. I was crazy in love. I had loved you for so long that when we finally got together, I thought my life couldn't be more perfect." Ry glanced down to see his hands were shaking, and he jammed them into his pockets. "There was this guy. I picked him up on a murder charge months before we got together. The charge didn't stick and he was released. In a matter of weeks he was back in on another charge, but he walked again." He swore, remembering how smooth and calculating Koch was, how his eyes could look straight through a person. He turned to face Margo. "Koch decided to have a little fun with me and a few of the other cops."

"Koch?"

"Koch Menaro, that was his name," Ry explained. "He left a couple of death threats in my squad. At first I didn't think much of it. That kind of thing happens from time to time. Nothing came of it, and life went on. A couple of the other cops received threats, too. You and I got together a few months later and then three weeks later I found another death threat. So did each of the other cops. The chief decided we should put tails on our relatives because the threats mentioned family members."

"Those two men you had watching me. They were protecting me?"

"Yes. They were supposed to, but you kept ditching them and making me climb the walls." Ry started to pace. "I thought about how vulnerable you were, and your mother, too. Even Blu. As much as he and I were at odds, I didn't want anything to happen to him. It seemed I only had one choice left.'' He stopped and looked at her.

''Walk away.''

Ry didn't think it was going to be so hard to admit. Finally, he said, ''Yes. I thought maybe, if I walked away quick enough, Koch would never know about you and your family.''

''And?''

Ry laughed bitterly. ''And it worked. Koch was focusing on the other three cops first, he'd been busy staking out their houses, following their families. It was just a stroke of luck that he'd decided to come after me last. Two men lost family members before we caught up with him, and—''

Ry heard her suck in her breath, watched her set the coffee cup down and stand. ''But you caught him, right?''

''I got a tip from one of my snitches. He said Koch was planning to hit one of the officer's homes. The officer and his family had taken off, but his daughter had come home unexpectedly. Only it wasn't unexpected. Koch had sent her a letter and lured her home.''

''Oh, God.''

''We got there in time to deactivate the bomb. The girl was unharmed.''

The scene suddenly flashed into Ry's mind. He'd been totally taken by surprise when Koch stepped out of the shadows to face him. He was in the house by himself, making one last check before he went back to the stationhouse to file his report.

''Koch was in the house. He'd been there from the moment we arrived. He was wearing a dark coat and he was smiling. He had a package in his hand.

A brown paper package. It reminded me of the kind of paper your mother wrapped up fish in.''

Ry heard Margo gasp, saw her wrap her arms around herself. He squeezed his eyes shut. ''I thought he'd found out about you. I thought maybe…maybe he'd done something terrible to you or your mother. I went crazy and lunged at him. I don't think he expected that. We fought, and when I knocked him down, the package slipped from his hand. I went after him again and started beating on him. Suddenly he started screaming about a bomb, but I told him it was already defused. He said no, then pointed to the package on the floor. That's the first I knew there was a second bomb. I wasn't sure how much time was left, but by the look on Koch's face I knew there couldn't be much. He struggled to get to his feet. He was on his knees when I turned and ran. The place went up in flames just as I went through the door. I was pitched thirty feet.''

There was a long span of silence. Finally she said, ''And Koch?''

''Dead. Everyone said he was dead. That he hadn't gotten out. They said I was the only one who came through the door.'' Ry turned back to the window and stared out into the black night.

''But you weren't sure, were you?''

''I wanted a body, proof that the whole crazy nightmare was over. I went to your mother's house, saw you in the upstairs window.'' Ry shook his head. ''I thought of all the crazy things that could have happened. I thought about what it would have been like if you hadn't been there.''

''But I was there, and I was all right.''

Ry spun around. ''I needed a body to know it was

all over. I needed to know that Koch would never be able to come back and hurt you. They never found him. Nothing. The bomb leveled the house and destroyed everything. I had planned to tell you all of this once we'd caught him. I never meant to stay away from you indefinitely. When I'd come up with the idea to walk away from our relationship it wasn't supposed to be forever, it was supposed to be just until the case was solved and Koch was frying in hell. A month, maybe two, at the most. That seemed like a long time to be without you, but it could have been forever if Koch had learned about you. It didn't take much to convince myself that I had done the right thing and that I should keep on doing it.''

"Because there was no body to prove it was over.''

"Exactly. So I decided—''

"To walk away forever.''

Her voice sounded odd, frail. Ry ran his hands through his hair. "Your safety was top priority. Every time I weakened and thought about telling you the truth, I reminded myself of how I felt when I saw Koch holding that brown paper package. You're everything to me, baby. I couldn't take a chance that Koch was out there just waiting for me to start living again. If he'd managed to get out of that explosion…'' Ry shook his head. "I did whatever I could to keep myself separated from everyone I cared about. I even sold my half of the ranch in Texas.''

"Do you believe Koch is dead?''

Ry hesitated. "The chief reminded me the other day that it's been two years. He pointed out that if

Koch was alive, I would have known about it by
now. I guess I've been letting the ghosts from the
past determine the future.''

"And now?"

"The past few days have shown me that there's
no guarantee either of us will make it to the end of
next week. You were shot on DuBay Pier while I
was napping in the hammock on the veranda. Tomorrow I could eat a bullet.''

"Tell me about the pills."

Ry hated this part of his confession most of all.
It wasn't pretty having to admit you'd become a
worthless slob. Would Margo be able to understand
how low a man could sink? How low he'd sunk?

"Ry…"

"I was angry. I wanted a body, dammit. Without
a body it meant I could either gamble with your life
once more or learn to live without you. I made the
second choice, then had a hard time living with it.
I wasn't much good to anyone for a long time. I
didn't eat, didn't sleep. Almost lost my job.'' Ry
tried to smile, but he failed. "You see, baby, you
were my addiction, too. My life seemed worthless
without you in it. The chief tried to help, even my
old snitch came to visit me a few times. As a last
resort I started seeing a shrink. That's how I got
tangled up with the pills.''

She took a step toward him, a tentative one, her
eyes full of concern. "You got better, right? You
don't take the pills anymore, do you?"

"No, not anymore."

"So the shrink helped?"

"No."

"Then how—"

"Did I pull myself together?"

"Yes."

Ry studied the concern on her face. Would she understand? Well, he wouldn't know until he tried to explain. He reached out and touched her cheek. "You'd just gotten the job at the Toucan, and I forced myself to go watch you perform. I'd avoided you up to that point, so seating myself at a table that first night in the same room with you was one of the hardest things I've had to do. I expected to feel worse, sorry for myself afterward, but the crazy thing was, it made me feel better. Seeing you alive and smiling at all those people helped me realize that the sacrifice had been worth every lonely night I would spend for the rest of my life. And that night I found peace for the first time in an entire year. You see, I still had a part of you. I would always have a part of you."

She was visibly shaking. Ry pulled her into his arms and held her. "Easy, baby, I didn't tell you this to upset you. I only—"

She pulled out of his arms. "Don't. Don't confuse me."

"What do you mean, confuse you? What I thought I was doing was clearing the air." Ry suddenly felt his hopes being flushed down the toilet. "Are you telling me it's too late?"

"I don't know."

"Are you saying Brodie's the man you want in your life?"

"I don't know."

"You loved me once."

Visibly angry, she shook her head. "Do you think love is just something a person turns on and off?"

"No, of course not. I knew you would need time to—"

"To fall helplessly in love with you a second time?"

"I admit I like the sound of that. Yes, I'd like that a lot."

"You should have told me the truth, damn you! You should have trusted me enough to play fair and let me make my own decision."

"Secrecy was important to keep Koch away from you. I did what I had to do. I still believe it was the best insurance I could buy at the time. I'm not visiting the cemetery like the others." Ry reached out and tried to pull her back into his arms, but she eluded him. "Margo, I know this wasn't an easy thing to hear. I'm sorry for all the pain I caused you, but maybe now—"

"We could have gone away. Disappeared. We could have—"

"Run. I thought about it. But Rose was still here, Blu, too. They would have been left behind, possibly hurt, and Koch would have still won."

"You have an answer for everything don't you?" She turned and headed out the door.

"Where are you going?"

"I need some air. Don't follow."

He let her go. Maybe she was right, maybe she needed time to absorb everything he'd said. He heard her footsteps on the stairs, heard the back door slam. Restless, he went looking for a cigarette. He'd give her ten minutes, he decided, ten minutes and then…

Ry tossed the unlit cigarette to the floor and bolted through the door.

Chapter 12

He found her in the swing between the two giant oak trees in the backyard. She was just sitting there with her knees drawn up and her head pressed against them. He didn't wait for an invitation. He simply sat down beside her, put his arm around her and pulled her close.

She didn't fight him, and Ry wasn't sure if that was good or bad. He started to move the swing in a slow, even rhythm. A moment later she dropped her feet to the ground and leaned against him.

"You know, I bought this place a year ago, just after I started going to the Toucan to see you. I remembered you telling me that when you were a kid you wanted a backyard with a swing in it. I didn't buy this place for the house or the neighborhood. They're nice enough, but—when I came to look at the place, I saw the swing in this quiet backyard and told the Realtor I'd take it. She wanted to show me the inside of the house, and I let her, but I wasn't really paying attention to the size or the number of bedrooms. All I wanted was the swing and the backyard.''

"The house is very pretty," she said softly.

"It's well built," Ry assured. "I admit the veranda interested me some because as a kid we had an old hammock on the front porch of the ranch house. My mama used to flog me out of it at the lazy age of fifteen. She must have used her broom on me at least twice a week."

Ry lowered his head and kissed Margo on the temple. "After work, I come here and imagine you sitting beside me. Sometimes I sleep on the veranda in the hammock and pretend you watch me from here."

"Please stop." She buried her face against his chest.

Ry lifted her chin. "No, I'm not going to stop. I'm going to keep telling you all the things that I thought about, all the things I did to keep myself sane. I couldn't be with you in the flesh, so I kept you close in my mind. I imagined us sitting here talking, and when the talking ran out, I envisioned you asking me to make love to you in the grass."

"Do you know how crazy that sounds?"

"Sure I do. Hell, the shrink confirmed it. But the fact is, it worked when the pills and the booze didn't. I've replayed those dreams over and over in my mind. We've made love in every room inside the house, and on every inch of this backyard. Seeing you three nights a week at the Toucan, singing those pretty songs to me—"

"To you?"

Ry heard the mix of surprise and amusement in her voice. "Yes, to me. They were all for me. I decided that at the very beginning." Ry lowered his head and kissed her gently. "What you have to believe, baby, is I loved you then and love you still. Hell broke loose, and we got caught in the middle of it. It was my fault. Understand, I take full responsibility for that, but now we have a chance to start over again. I want to believe Koch is dead. I should have believed it from the beginning."

"You make it sound so easy. It's not."

Ry felt a huge lump close off his throat. Forcing himself to swallow, he said, "I want you here. Move in with me, baby." He closed his eyes, waited for her to say something. She didn't.

The night air was warm, the fragrant jasmine drifting on the gentle breeze. Minutes passed. Finally she said, "Remember when you asked me if I was sleeping with Brodie. I want you to know that—"

"He hasn't touched you."

She sat up quickly, gazed at him. "How did you know?"

Ry kept the swing moving, kept his arm on her shoulder. "I remember everything." He smiled down at her. "I especially like those crazy little sounds you make when you first feel me inside you, the way you twist to the right just a fraction, then arch up like..." He stopped himself from going on, and asked what he already knew, or at least suspected. "You've never made love to anyone else but me, have you?"

Her chin went up. "It wasn't because no one

asked, so don't think—I had plenty of—Brodie wanted to—''

Ry pulled her close and kissed her quiet. ''You haven't slept with anyone for the same reason I haven't. There was no point.''

''What are you saying?''

Ry stopped the swing. ''I'm saying I love you, Margo duFray. I have and will until the day I die. I'm saying there was no reason to bring someone else into the picture when you were all I ever wanted.''

Her look of disbelief bothered him. ''Look, I had plenty of opportunities, too. I just didn't act on any of them.'' When her bewildered look remained, Ry removed his arm from around her and stood.

''Where are you going?''

Ry headed for the back door. Over his shoulder, he said, ''Upstairs.''

He kept moving, kept hoping he would hear the swing creak, that she'd follow him. On the veranda he stopped and looked back; she was still sitting in the swing. He forced himself inside, the door banging behind him. He was in the hall when he heard footsteps rushing the stairs. She caught up with him just as he stepped through the bedroom doorway. A little out of breath, she sighed, ''Chastity for you, Ry... Do you expect me to believe you deprived yourself of a woman's—''

''Touch...'' He turned quickly, pulled her through the door and into the bedroom. ''Yes, I do expect you to believe me. But in case you're in doubt, tell me what I can do to convince you.'' He backed her against the door and felt her tremble. He lowered his head and kissed her, kissed her until she was breathless and clinging to him.

"Wait," Margo sighed, then reached for the buttons on his shirt. As she peeled Ry's shirt from his shoulders, the moonlight shining through the window danced around them. "Now me," she entreated and sank against the closed door. Her heart was pounding as he opened her shirt and spread it wide.

Margo watched him lower his head, knew she would be unable to hold back, and moaned the moment she felt his lips on her breast. She reached up to hold his head in place as he continued to worship her with his tongue. His hands moved over her hips, lower to her sheer white panties. Then he was on his knees, trailing kisses down her flat belly, along the elastic edge of her panties, his tongue teasing her through the sheer fabric.

"Oh, Ry…"

"You're so beautiful," he whispered, the heat from his mouth driving her crazy, his fingers adding another element of pleasure as they worked their way up the back of her legs and into her panties to gently knead her backside.

"I used to dream of this," he confessed, his hands adoring her with gentle persuasion. "It made me so hard." Margo shivered, offered a quick intake of breath. "Did you dream of me, baby?" he asked.

Surprised by the question, Margo hesitated. When his hands stilled, she looked down and found his blue eyes assessing her, waiting for an answer. She tried to speak. When she couldn't, she looked away.

"Tell me I wasn't the only one having sex with a memory. Tell me I slept with you sometimes, made love to you in your bedroom in the middle of the night. Admit when you touched yourself you pretended it was me touching you.'' He got back to his feet, turned her head so he could look into her eyes.

Margo's cheeks grew hot. ''Yes,'' she finally confessed. ''Yes, I dreamed of you, and, yes, you touched me in my dreams.''

Instead of telling her how much her admission pleased him, he showed her by taking her lips with a desperate moan. Margo let him control the kiss, but when he pulled away to catch his breath, she slid her hands down his chest to fondle him through his jeans. While he groaned out his pleasure, she changed places with him and pushed him against the wall. Again she caressed him through his jeans, her fingers working the snap open, then his zipper.

Her fingers found him hot and hard, and she possessively ran her thumb over the end of him. He groaned and held on until he couldn't stand it any longer, then he was suddenly taking back the control and lifting her into his arms. As he carried her to the bed, he whispered, ''No more pretending, no more imagining.''

He laid her on the bed, then removed his boots and jeans. Naked, all bronzed and hard like a prized statue who deserved a private exhibition, he loomed over her. Margo marveled at the sight of his perfection.

He quickly joined her on the bed and pulled her close. ''I've got one more thing to tell you.''

Margo stiffened. ''Something more? Do I want to know?''

''It's not bad.''

''Then tell me.''

"It's about this house. It's really not mine."

"What do you mean? You said you bought it."

"I did, but the deed is in your name. It's really your house."

His confession rendered Margo speechless. Then the tears came.

"Oh, baby, don't cry."

"I can cry if I want to," Margo sniffed unable to stop. She struggled to sit up. "What am I going to do with you? You can't love someone that much. You didn't even know if we would ever talk to each other again, let alone—"

"Shhh." He rolled onto his back and tugged her on top of him.

Margo squirmed until she was straddling him. "I suppose you want to hear my confession now."

"Do you have one?"

"The truth is, I have a scrapbook. I started it before you ever kissed me. Actually, I think I bought it the week we first met. I thought you were so sexy and cute. Every time I saw your name in the newspaper, I cut it out and pasted it in my scrapbook."

She watched him as her words registered.

"Are you telling me—"

"Yes. I'm saying I wanted you in the beginning. I was fifteen and—"

He didn't allow her to finish. He rolled quickly and placed her beneath him. He kissed her long and hard. Kissed her until they were both panting, both burning. Then he was inside her, silently promising her forever.

Ry stood on the veranda and listened to Jackson recap the past four hours. It was two in the morning, and Margo was asleep upstairs. They'd made love for several hours, and when she'd finally fallen asleep in his arms, he had slipped away quietly and called his partner.

"You were right," Jackson said, "that piece of garbage in the locker could be important." He pulled the paper from his back pocket and handed it to Ry. "The boat is named the *Dungeress*. She's older than my grandmother, but she's still in port and in one piece. Some activist group is claiming she's got historical value. The city's agreed to hold off scrapping her until they can decide if she'd be worth renovating."

"Where's she at?" Ry asked as he scanned the wrinkled newspaper article.

"That's the interesting part. She's docked in River Bay, just west of where Blu duFray docks his Devils. And there's something else. Less than a block away is a warehouse owned by Denoux Inc."

Ry's ears perked up. "Wasn't that where our floater worked?"

"You got it." Jackson yawned and eased his body into the hammock.

Ry mulled over the information, then said, "Did you check out the company?"

"Yeah." Jackson folded his arms behind his head. "They look legit, but that means nothing. A big company that size could front all kinds of illegal activity."

"How big?"

"That's what took me so long. I went back to the stationhouse to get a profile. They've got an office in Honduras, Rio de Janeiro and Monaco. They're

an import-export that deals in everything from to-
bacco to tennis shoes.''

Ry checked his watch. Margo was likely to sleep
the entire night. If he had luck on his side, he'd be
back before morning, and she wouldn't even know
he'd stepped out. ''Margo will probably sleep
through the night.''

''Sure about that, are you?''

Jackson's light tone had Ry looking up to see his
partner grinning. ''What does that mean?''

Jackson wiggled himself into a more comfortable
position and crossed his jeans-clad legs. Yawned.
''You look like a man who's just had the weight of
the world lifted off your shoulders. You're not digging in your pockets for a smoke, or pacing. Some
would call them nasty habits. Me, I always saw them
as acquired obsessions to counter another.'' He
paused, his grin holding. ''Is Margo duFray your
obsession, partner?''

Ry gazed at the swing in the backyard. ''For
about five years,'' he admitted.

''That would have made her…''

''Too damn young for me to be looking. Yeah, I
know. But it wasn't until a few years ago that I did
anything about it.'' Ry turned and leaned against the
iron rail. ''I love her, Jackson, but it's a long story.
Tonight, what I need from you is what I've been
getting the past couple of days. I want you to keep
Margo safe while I check out the *Dungeress*. I'll be
back as quickly as I can, hopefully with some answers.''

Ry drove past DuBay Pier and parked his Blazer
two blocks away from River Bay. As he walked to-

ward the waterfront he spotted the *Dungeress*. She
was an old relic, her twin outriggers half-gone, the
stabilizers shot. She looked ravaged by time and
weather, but she still had her nets hanging. She was
big for a trawler, at least eighty feet long, and made
of solid wood. Ry had no idea if the boat had his-
toric value, but right now he didn't care as long as
it led him to Mickey's killer.

The night was balmy, the water calm, the sky dot-
ted with a million and one stars. Quietly he boarded
the shrimper, pulling his gun from his holster as he
crept around the wheelhouse. Slowly he opened the
door to the hold. The steps creaked and groaned as
he took them one at a time. Halfway down the stairs,
Ry sensed he wasn't alone.

"It took you long enough."

He recognized the voice, but it lacked the built-
in arrogance Blu duFray had been born with.

Ry took another step, then another, until the stairs
ran out and he was standing in total darkness in the
bowels of the *Dungeress*. Suddenly a light snapped
on in a far corner. The bright light made Ry squint,
but he could still make out Blu sprawled on the
floor, his back braced against the wall. He looked
like hell his face dirty and his shaggy, black hair
matted.

He moved closer, and when he saw Margo's
brother's leg, he said, "Holy hell, Blu. You should
be in the hospital."

"*Oui*. I should be. I'll get there eventually. That
is, if you're as good a detective as the city seems to
think you are."

"The clue you left in the locker wasn't much to

go on, and your sister's damn stubborn when she's protecting Saint Blu.''

The comment brought a smile to Blu's face. "Then she's all right?"

"She's fine. Worried about you, but doing okay."

It looked like the weight of the world had been lifted off Blu's shoulders. Ry was aware of it, but this time he felt no jealousy. He would never understand this fierce sibling connection Margo and Blu shared, but he was ready to accept it.

He knelt down to examine Blu's leg. The infection was raging. It had to hurt like hell. Blu needed a doctor as soon as possible.

"Did you bring the cavalry?" Blu asked.

"No. I wasn't sure what I'd find. I'm alone. Come on, Blu, lets get you out of this place."

Blu reached out and gripped Ry's arm. "No, not until we've talked."

Ry heard a noise from behind him, and as he turned, Blu shone the light into the opposite corner. Goddard Reese sat on the floor, his arms bound with a rope that had been skillfully looped around his ankles to keep him hobbled. He was also gagged.

"Is he yours?" Blu asked.

"Yeah, he's mine."

"That's what he said, but I couldn't be sure, so Mort tied him up."

"Mort?" Ry heard another noise and Blu sent the flashlight around the room to another corner, and there, huddled together, were a half dozen wide-eyed dirty kids. "The oldest, she's seventeen," Blu said, shining the spotlight on a young girl who kept her head lowered. Beside her a small girl lay curled up with her head in the older girl's lap. "She's the youngest, maybe eight."

A moment later the sound of footsteps on the creaky stairs sent Ry after his gun.

"That would be Mort," Blu said. "He's my watchdog." He moved the light toward the stairs, and sure enough another ragged-looking kid, this one maybe sixteen, came into focus.

"You all right?" Mort asked Blu. "He looked like the man you described, that's why I let him pass."

"You did good, Mort. He's the one."

Noise in the other corner reminded Ry that Goddard was still tied up. He stood, took the flashlight from Blu and went to release the older man. Once he'd stripped the gag and freed Goddard's arms and legs, the old man said, "that one," he pointed to Mort, "he hit me over the head and tied me up." The older man rubbed an area at the back of his head. "That was yesterday morning. Where the hell you been, Superman? This place ain't fit for pigs."

Grinning, Ry stuffed the butt of the flashlight in his back pocket, then pulled a fifty out of his wallet and stuffed it in Goddard's shirt pocket. "I told you you'd get a bonus if you found Blu. There it is." He helped the older man up. "Now go on. I'll look you up in a few days."

"Make it a week. It's gonna take me that long to get rid of this headache."

As God shuffled toward the stairs, he said, "What you gonna do with the merchandise? Blu says these kids are it."

It was what Ry suspected the minute he saw the children. The thought sickened him, and he said loud enough so they could hear. "They're going back to their families as soon as we can figure out who they are and where they belong. Go on, old man. I got work to do." Once Goddard was gone, Ry turned his attention on Mort. "Come and hold this light."

While Mort did as he was told, Ry went around and checked the children. For the most part, they were unharmed. They were dirty and scared as hell, but Blu had done his best to keep them fed—there was food wrappers on the floor.

Ry counted six of them, four girls and two boys counting Mort. He returned to Blu. "So what's the story?"

"Taber Denoux is a white slave runner, that's the story," Blu growled. "He smuggles kids out of the country hidden in his cargo. I stumbled on the kids by accident."

"And how did Mickey Burelly fit in?" Ry asked.

"He really didn't," Blu sighed. "I knew him from a few months back. When he arrived in town, Mickey had racked up a pile of bills. As they say, he was a little man digging with a big auger. He ended up borrowing money from Patch Pollaro, and that's how we met. He was late on a payment and I was sent to remind him how the system worked. When I saw the kids that night, I knew what was going on. I thought about walking away, then about dumping them at the precinct. I ended up stashing them here. I wasn't sure who the big man was running the operation and—"

"You weren't so sure Pollaro wasn't involved," Ry finished. "And if he had been?"

"I don't know. By the time I learned that he

wasn't, I learned who was. I thought it would be better if I just passed the kids off to Mickey Burelly. I knew him, and it fit into my plan to remain anonymous. I called him and set up a meeting. Then to make sure things didn't fall apart, I put that newspaper article about the shrimper in the locker for insurance. I planned on mailing the key to the precinct if Mickey didn't live up to his promise and get the kids back to their folks."

"You should have called me," Ry insisted.

"Too many people know me on the waterfront. I didn't want the publicity. And you know as well as I do when this story breaks it'll be big news."

"Afraid it's going to make you look like one of the good guys?" Ry couldn't hide his amusement. "If that happens, Patch Pollaro won't have any use for your talent, right?"

"I don't enjoy working for Patch. I'm a fisherman, Ry, that's what I do. Breaking a few noses and fingers along the way keeps the Devils on the water. But I won't have to do it for much longer."

"If you need money so bad, why not sell the kids?" Ry taunted.

Blu swore. "The men I deal with aren't innocent victims, old man. I might walk a fine line, but I'm no criminal. Those kids have done nothing to be here. They don't deserve any of this."

"Well, I'll take it from here."

"No, you won't," Blu snapped. "My sister was nearly killed, and I'm carrying lead in my leg. Taber Denoux is going to pay for what he's done. From here on out we work as a team."

"You need to go to the hospital, Blu."

"I'm not going anywhere until we get Denoux, and my kids are back where they belong."

Shocked to hear Blu's claim on the kids, Ry studied Margo's brother.

"What?" Blu rested his head against the wall and closed his eyes. "What are you grinning at?"

"You. Margo was right. She said there was a soft side to you. I never saw it, not until now. I guess maybe that's because I was too busy not liking you before, to give you a chance."

"Didn't like you much, either." Blu's dark eyes, a perfect match to his sister's, opened to stare back at Ry. "So what's the plan, old man? I want a piece of Denoux for Margo and a piece for each one of my kids."

"We'll split him up," Ry promised. "Now, let's get you on your feet."

Chapter 13

Margo woke with a start and sat up quickly. Ry was no longer beside her, she sensed it before she actually ran her hand over the cool sheets beside her. Thinking he stood at the window, she let the sheet fall and was about to slip off the bed when the man at the window spoke. "You truly are beautiful, even when you sleep."

Margo gasped, then snatched up the sheet and covered her naked breasts. "Who are you?"

The stranger moved out of the shadows, and as he did, the moonlight revealed his face. "I know you," Margo stammered. "You're the pirate from the Toucan tonight. The man at the back door."

"Pirate?" An amused smile touched his thin lips. "My name is Taber Denoux."

Margo didn't recognize the name. Should she? "Where's Ry?"

"You should have taken me up on my offer to

escort you home. If you had, your friend downstairs would still be alive.''

"No. No!''

"It wasn't Archard. It was the other one.''

Margo struggled for air. "Jackson? You've killed Jackson. Oh, God!''

"We can't keep them all alive, *Beautiful.*'' He eased down on the bed beside her, and Margo recoiled, clutching the sheet tighter. "You really are stunning, you know. Perfection is hard to find these days. Perfection and loyalty. Owning something as extraordinary as you—well, let's just say it's not every day a man can make his fantasy come true.''

Margo ignored his words. "Where's Blu?''

"Until a few hours ago, I couldn't have answered that. But Archard led my men to him about an hour ago.''

"Ry knows where Blu is?''

"So it seems. Didn't he tell you?''

Margo was confused. If Ry knew where Blu was, he would have told her. Wouldn't he?

"How do you feel about tropical beaches and margaritas?''

"What?''

"We're taking a little trip, you and I. Which will it be, a warm beach or a mountain retreat?''

"You killed Mickey Burelly.''

"In a roundabout way I suppose that's true. I didn't actually pull the trigger, but...'' He shrugged, smiled. "You've been a very elusive little bird, my dear. I'll have to decide what form of punishment you deserve for my trouble.''

Margo shivered beneath the sheet.

"Oh, don't worry. It won't be anything that

would mar your perfection." He reached out and traced the length of Margo's long neck with one finger. "As I said, you're a rare beauty. But I can't have you rebelling against me anytime you feel like it. So be warned. I can hurt you in other ways far more satisfying for me and much more degrading for you."

He was an animal in an expensive suit, Margo decided, but an animal nonetheless. "You destroyed my apartment."

"You'll have no need for that tawdry wardrobe. I've bought you a new one." He stood, his black suit and long hair making him appear as sinister as he truly was. "Come, let me help you dress for our trip."

"Go to hell."

He raised an eyebrow. "Careful. Your brother and Archard are not dead yet. My men are watching them at this precise moment, waiting for my instructions."

"You're crazy."

"No, you are, if you think you can fight me and win. If you don't come with me, and I don't make a phone call to my men within the hour, they have orders to kill your brother, then Archard."

"How can I trust you?"

He reached for an elegant white dress that was draped over the back of the paisley chair. Margo focused on it, wondered why she hadn't noticed it sooner. "I don't see that you have much choice."

He could be bluffing, but what if he wasn't? "If I go with you, you'll let them both live?"

He handed her the dress. "The only promise I can

make is that they'll be dead within the hour if you don't. Put it on.''

Margo snatched the dress from him. ''Turn your back.''

He smiled, then slowly turned away from her. Quickly Margo dropped the sheet and slipped off the bed. She wiggled into the shift in record time, then glanced down seeing how the expensive dress accented every curve she owned.

''Perfect,'' he admired.

Margo glanced up quickly, watched as Taber Denoux pulled a pair of white satin panties from his pocket. ''Now these.'' When she made no move to reach for them, he sighed. ''Put them on, or come as you are. But you will come, or your brother and Archard will die like the cop downstairs.''

Margo snatched the panties from him and discreetly worked them up her legs, careful that he saw only the bare minimum.

''Modest, too. You really are a treasure.'' He bent down and scooped up a pair of white shoes that sat beside the chair. ''Now these.''

This time Margo didn't hesitate—she took the sandals and slipped them on. ''You won't get away with this. You might think so, but Ry Archard is the best detective in the city. He'll track you down.''

Taber Denoux forced Margo down the stairs ahead of him. And once she'd reached the kitchen, a man was waiting for them by the door. He was well over six feet tall, an ominous-looking man with light-colored, cropped hair in a military style that made him look as mean as it did capable. He wore a suit as expensive and dark as Taber Denoux's.

"This is Gino, my new man," he told her. "His job is simple, to keep me happy."

The big man opened the back door and steered Margo onto the veranda. And that's when she saw Jackson Ward laying lifeless in the hammock.

Ry managed to get Blu to his feet with Mort's help. As bad off as Blu's leg was, Ry realized Margo's brother wasn't going to the hospital until he was sure *his* kids were safe and Denoux was caught.

Ry propped Blu against the wall and had just turned around when he heard a noise overhead.

"Superman…"

Ry watched as Goddard Reese, tripping over his feet, hurried back down the stairs. "What the hell, old man. I thought I told you—"

"We got company," he interrupted. "There's two of 'um on the waterfront. They're packin' serious noisemakers, too."

"Did they see you?"

"No."

Blu swore. "They must have followed you, Ry."

If that was true, then they had been watching the house, and before that, Margo at the Toucan. For one quick minute Ry wanted to head back and make sure Margo was all right, but then he told himself that the men outside were looking for Blu and the children, not Margo. She was perfectly safe with Jackson watching over her.

He headed for the stairs.

"Where are you going?" Blu asked.

"I'm going to check out the situation."

"I'm coming with you," Blu insisted.

"They got us pinned." Goddard wrapped his coat around himself. "Ain't no way off this boat. No, sir. Not unless you can swim, and I can't."

"I could divert them." The rough voice came from Mort. He stepped forward. "I come and go. Food runs, mostly, but I know how to get off the boat without anyone seeing me. Once I'm off, I could—"

"No!" Blu shoved away from the wall and stood on his own power for the first time in four days. "You stay with the kids, Mort. If I don't come back, the old man here," he grabbed Goddard by the sleeve and shoved him forward, "he'll make sure you get to the stationhouse."

"The hell I will."

Ry turned and nailed Goddard with a hard look. "The hell you won't."

Goddard jerked away from Blu. "But, Superman—"

"We're wasting time," Blu growled, hobbling toward the stairs. "Me first," he told Ry. "That way if I lose my balance, you can break my fall."

Blu's light banter and his ghost of a smile had Ry taking a second look at Margo's brother. He decided the Blu Devil even had a sense of humor.

They surfaced from the hold moments later, both belly crawling across the deck. Ry scanned the waterfront and easily spotted the two men. He watched as one of the men played with his automatic weapon, while the other man started onto the pier.

He motioned to Blu, then pointed to the jiggler chains hanging from the nets. Ry let him know what his intentions were, then ordered Blu to stay put. A moment later he was at the nets on the far side of the boat. The chains were sturdy, and he grabbed hold of one of them and, hand-over-hand, lowered himself into the water.

Barely making a ripple in the water, Ry swam to the pier and ducked under it. He could hear the man walking a short distance away. Carefully he positioned himself and waited. The slatted deck boards weren't wide enough for his hand to slip through, so Ry knew what he would have to do.

When the time came to make his move, Ry did it quickly. He rose out of the water like a dragon in the mist and gripped the man's leg where he stood gazing at the stars. The man screamed in surprise, but before he could move, Ry was jerking him off balance. The man tumbled into the water with a hard splash. Ry knocked his victim out quickly, then hauled him beneath the pier.

He heard the other man holler, heard him running to see what had happened. Ry rolled over the unconscious man and gave him a solid shove away from the pier. The running overhead stopped suddenly. "Rudy? Rudy, if you've went and got yourself killed, I'll shoot you. Rudy!"

Silence.

"There you are. Stop clowning around, Rudy. Rudy!"

Ry didn't understand why Blu choose that moment to stand up, but if he was trying to be a diversion, it worked. The man on the pier noticed the movement and spun halfway around and shot at Blu.

Ry saw Blu dive for cover, and as the man drew up to shoot again, he rose out of the water once more and peeled the gunman off the pier quick and easy.

A few well-placed punches, and the man was floating beside his unconscious friend.

The sound of a boat moving in fast caught Ry's attention, and by the time the *Nightwing* came into sight, Blu was already hobbling off the *Dungeress* expecting to see his foreman, Brodie Hewitt. But the man who steered the cruiser alongside the pier turned out to be Jackson Ward.

Ry quickly hauled himself onto the pier. "What the hell are you doing here? Where's Margo?" A quick search of the cruiser told him she wasn't there. "Is she still at the house? How did you get this boat out of impound?"

"I stole it," Jackson admitted. "Get in!"

"You what! Holy hell!"

"Just get your ass in the boat. I know what I'm doing."

"You better know what the hell you're doing," Ry warned, "now answer me. Is Margo at home?"

"No, by now she's probably on Denoux's yacht." Jackson pointed to the hole in his shirt. "I'd be a dead man right now if I hadn't worn my bulletproof vest tonight. It's a damn good thing that hulk Denoux had with him didn't aim for my head."

"Well, that's where I'm going to be aiming if anything happens to Margo," Ry warned as he jumped into the cruiser. When he turned around and saw Blu struggling to get into the boat, he reached over and hauled Margo's brother over the rail. "Let's go, Jackson!"

Before Jackson could respond, Blu took the wheel and spun the *Nightwing* away from the pier with one expert flick of his wrist. Then they were streaking across the river, headed for the Gulf.

"Do you know where you're going?" Ry yelled.

For an answer Blu hauled back on the accelerator and turned up the speed.

Brodie looked awful, but he was alive.

Margo jerked away from Taber Denoux and rushed to her friend's side and dropped down beside him. "Brodie, it's me. It's Margo."

"Margo?" He opened his swollen eyes, his face a mass of bruises. "Hey, sweet thing, you okay?"

"Don't worry about me." She scrambled back to her feet. "I want him untied now! And I want him off this boat."

Taber Denoux reached out and pulled Margo up against him. It was the first time he had used any kind of physical force with her. "Yacht, Beautiful. They call this a yacht, not a boat. An expensive yacht."

Margo didn't give a damn what it was called or how expensive it was. All she knew was that it was leaving port that very minute, and Brodie's and her escape route would be cut off.

Taber smiled, then glanced down at Brodie. "Are you intending to bargain for this man's life, too?" He shook his head, pulled her closer. "I'm not surprised. You seem to think you're responsible for everyone's well-being." He released her arm to stroke her bare shoulder. "Very soon the only one you're going to need to concern yourself with is me."

Margo knocked his hand away, and he allowed her her freedom. "That won't happen!"

"Is Hewitt just a friend or a lover like Archard?"

"He's a friend. An innocent friend who doesn't

deserve to be here.'' Margo knelt beside Brodie once more. ''I'll get you out of here,'' she promised, wiping the blood out of his eyes and purposely on the white dress she was wearing.

''What he just said about Archard. Is he... Are you back with him?''

Margo hesitated. ''Brodie, you know I—''

''Shhh. You could never forget him. I know. It's all right, sweet thing. I knew what the odds were going in. I've always known.''

Margo felt Taber's hand on her shoulder, and she tried to pull away, but his grip turned to iron, and he hauled her up to face him. ''He's filthy. I don't want you touching him. He'll soil your...'' He spied the blood. ''You've ruined the dress.''

''I don't care about your stupid dress,'' Margo spat. ''I want Brodie off this *boat*. I want him unharmed, along with Blu and Ryland Archard. If you agree, I'll go wherever you want, and I'll go willingly.''

She heard Brodie protest behind her. Heard him thrash against his ropes. Gino walked past her and gave him several hard kicks to the midsection.

''Stop that!'' Margo turned toward Brodie, but Taber jerked her back.

''You have no bargaining power now, my little songbird. You are here, and here is where you'll stay. But you are right about one thing. Hewitt is no longer of value. Gino, she wants him off the yacht, so give her what she wants.''

To Margo's horror, she watched Gino and three other men hoist Brodie, tied to a deadhead, up and toss him overboard. ''No! No!''

Margo tried to follow Brodie into the water, but

she was restrained by Taber's solid grip. Holding her fast, he said, "I don't make deals when I'm holding all the cards. Willing or not, you're mine now." He turned to the hulk who was grinning stupidly. "Gino, I want her locked in my stateroom. She's as resourceful as she is beautiful. Remember that."

The giant nodded, and Margo's stomach knotted as he hauled her away and forced her below deck. He swung the door open to Taber's home away from home and shoved her inside. The elaborate stateroom was decorated all in white and polished brass, and as elegant as the white dress he'd insisted she put on a few hours ago.

When Margo heard the door lock behind her, she sagged against the wall. She tried to get past feeling sorry for herself, but she was afraid. They were already miles from shore. She needed a new plan of escape, but she didn't have one.

Her thoughts turned to Brodie and Jackson, and she started to cry. Minutes later she was wiping her tears and pulling up her chin. She could either fall apart, which she was very close to doing, or she could make use of the time she had alone to look for something that might help her escape when the time came.

Quickly, she began to tear the stateroom apart, searching for something that might prove useful. She found the small porthole windows by accident. They were hidden behind elegant white panels of silk. Small in size, they were too narrow to pass through for a woman with hips, but Margo didn't have any hips, something she was suddenly thankful for.

She sucked in her breath, as a shred of hope sent her ripping at the silk panels. When she tried the window latch and found it locked, she ripped at another panel of silk and tried another. The fourth window was the prize, or so she thought. Margo flung the window open and was confronted with an endless body of churning blackness.

Oh, God…

She stepped back and squeezed her eyes shut. She hated water, hated the uncertainty. No, this wasn't an escape route, this was suicide.

She heard a key being inserted in the door and turned to find Taber stepping into the room. When he saw what she was about to do, he rushed at her and half pulled, half tackled her to the floor. Margo went down hard, and for a moment the wind was knocked out of her. It was enough time for Taber to get the upper hand and pin her beneath him.

When she could breathe again, he was straddling her, looming over her with a smile on his face. "No," she refused when his lips took hers.

"Either way I'm going to have you. Why not make it easier on yourself? Why not learn to like me?"

"Never." Margo spit in his face and when he lifted his hand to wipe it away, she shot her fist into his abdomen and drove upward. It was a maneuver Blu had taught her to defend herself, and it worked beautifully. It rendered Taber Denoux speechless, then stole his balance. As he fell over and rolled onto his back, Margo scrambled to her feet. She was on her way back to the porthole, when she stopped in midstride and hurried back to Taber where he lay gasping for air. Without hesitation, she hauled back and kicked the man in the groin. "That's for destroying my plants, you heartless bastard."

Poised at the porthole once more, Margo started

to shake, then her knees turned to putty. On unsteady limbs, she peered through the opening once more. All she had to do was wiggle through the hole and drop twenty feet into the black water of the Gulf while the yacht sped away, leaving her in the middle of nowhere. Simple, right?

It didn't take Margo long to convince herself it was the craziest idea she'd ever contemplated. Two minutes later, she kicked off her shoes.

"What the hell is that?"

"What?"

Jackson pointed to a log floating in the water.

"Hey, Brodie," Blu holler, "You alive, *mon ami?*"

Moments later, Ry was in the water, untying Brodie from the massive deadhead and helping him into the boat. "Denoux's got Margo," he puffed breathlessly as he tumbled onto the deck. "He's taking her with him to some island." He locked gazes with Ry. "You're getting a second chance, I hear. Don't blow it, or it'll be your last."

"Take it easy," Blu said. "Jackson, get Brodie below and—"

"No way, I'm staying up top. Just get moving. That yacht can't be more than a few miles ahead of us."

Brodie was right. Minutes later they spotted Taber's yacht in the moonlight.

"There she is," Jackson said.

Ry's eyes locked on the yacht, and a million emotions caught him by the throat. It was as if the past was rising up to taunt him. He felt angry, guilty, most of all, scared. After two years, just when they had managed to put the past behind them, another crazy man was trying to steal his and Margo's happiness. Well, not this time, Ry promised silently. He wouldn't let it happen. He wasn't going to allow anything or anyone to take Margo away from him a second time.

"Call the Coast Guard," he growled. Then to Brodie he said, "You're sure she was all right?"

"She's not hurt," Brodie confirmed. "At least not yet."

Once more, Ry scanned the yacht. He wouldn't be able to board until the Coast Guard showed up. Be patient, he told himself. As long as they had her in sight, they would—

"What's that?"

Ry jerked his attention in the direction Jackson was pointing. "See it, that streak of white."

"She wouldn't," Ry muttered, suddenly afraid to contemplate what was half hanging out of the porthole of Denoux's yacht. "She wouldn't be that reckless."

"Oh, I don't know. Chaining you to the bed was pretty gutsy."

"Shut up, Jackson."

Blu motioned for Brodie to take over the wheel, then produced a pair of night vision binoculars and zeroed in on the porthole. "Hell, yes, that's Chili." He watched a second longer, then shook his head. "She won't do it. She won't jump into the water from that height. She hates the water. She won't jump," he assured Ry. Then suddenly he knocked Brodie away from the wheel and increased their speed.

"I thought you said she wouldn't jump," Ry growled sensing Blu was in a damn big hurry all of a sudden.

"Maybe she's got more to live for today than she

did four days ago. You tell her why you walked out on her?''

Ry jerked his head toward Blu. "You know why?"

"Sure, I know why. You didn't think I would let you get away with hurting my sister without getting even, did you? I'd have killed you and fed you to the fish if the lie you told her had been the truth. So did you? Did you tell her you still love her? Does she know you walked away to protect her?"

"To protect her?" Brodie was suddenly all ears.

"Are we going to have to share her with a cop again?" Blu pressed. "Are you back in my sister's life, old man?"

"I bought her a house," Ry said, as if that explained his intentions, or why Margo would suddenly consider diving out a window headfirst into the Gulf.

"Jesus, she's gonna do it!" Brodie yelled.

"Not gonna," Jackson amended. "She did it!"

Ry saw Margo disappear into the water headfirst and his heart leaped into his throat. Then he was kicking off his boots and ordering Brodie to turn on the floodlight to search the water.

As Taber Denoux's yacht sped away, Blu cut the *Nightwing*'s engine. The minute Ry saw Margo's head surface, he was in the water, swimming to her like a sprinter in a high-stake race. It seemed like forever before he reached her, but when he did, he pulled her close and squeezed her so tightly he swore he heard her bones protest. Then he said, "Are you all right?"

She pulled away smiling. "Now I am. If you're here, does that mean Blu's safe, too?"

''Yes. He's got a bum leg, but he's too ornery to let that get him down.''

Margo sobered. ''Jackson and Brodie are—''

''All right,'' Ry promised. ''We picked up Brodie a few minutes ago, and Jackson had a bulletproof vest on. He'll have a sore chest for a few days but nothing more.''

''Oh, Ry, that's wonderful!''

''Is it true?''

''Is what true?'' She asked, clinging to him.

''Is it true you have more to live for today than you did four days ago? Blu said you wouldn't jump. Not unless—''

''Do you think after what you told me tonight I was going to let Taber Denoux sail me off to some tropical island and wine and dine me with his fortune and live like a queen when I could have a backyard swing?''

''Margo…''

Laughing, she kissed him. ''Oh, I almost forgot the best part, shrimp in bed with the sexiest cop in New Orleans. Ry?''

''Yes.''

''Why is *our* kitchen all yellow?

''Because it's your favorite color.''

''Yellow? No, it's not. It's blue. It's always been blue, silly. The color of your eyes.''

For the middle of the night the precinct was still humming with activity. Ry escorted Margo to a chair, and she wrapped the blanket she'd gotten off the *Nightwing* around her chilled body and gladly sank onto the chair while Blu and Ry headed into Chief Blais's office.

She watched through the window as Ry and Blu explained what had taken place tonight and why. She was still a little overwhelmed by the whole story Blu had told her on the way to the precinct. Taber Denoux was in the business of stealing children and selling them to prospective buyers out of the country.

Margo shuddered and closed her eyes. She couldn't believe someone could do something so despicable. Moments ago, the Coast Guard had called in and said they had apprehended Taber Denoux and his men—it looked as though the pirate was going to get everything he deserved.

"You okay?"

Margo opened her eyes to see Blu sink down in the chair next to her. He looked so tired, so thin. "I'm fine. Are you finished in there so I can take you to the hospital?"

"I'm heading that way now. Jackson's going to drive me over. He's not too excited about explaining to Blais how he stole the *Nightwing* out of impound."

Margo glanced down at his leg. It looked horrible, and she was terribly afraid it was going to leave him with a severe limp or worse. "Do you think we should call Mama?"

"We'll call her in the morning. You wait for the old man." Blu leaned over and kissed Margo's forehead. "Thanks."

"Thanks?" She frowned. "For what?"

"For going to Ry's place the night you were shot. I know it was hard, but it's what made the difference. He saved the day, you know."

"But you saved the kids." Margo touched Blu's cheek. "I'm so proud of you."

"I couldn't leave them. They were so damn scared." Blu shook his head. "Denoux's a sick bastard."

"I'm told the kids' families have been called."

"Yeah, I heard."

Margo saw Jackson heading their way, a scruffy teenager walking a few steps behind him with his head down. "This one won't talk," he told Blu. "You sure he can speak?"

"He can speak," Blu assured. "What's up, Mort?"

"Nothing."

"So tell the man what he wants to know. Then you can get the hell out of here and go home."

"I don't have nothing to say. I'm not like the others." The kid shoved his hands into his pockets and stared at his shoes. Finally he said, "They got families and a home. I don't."

It suddenly turned quiet. Then Blu surprised Margo by standing and saying, "Well, you do now, Mort. That is, if you like sleeping on a boat."

"I'm not picky, sir."

"Blu. Call me Blu. I've never been a sir and never will be."

Margo watched her brother put his arm around Mort and head for the door with a profound limp. Over his shoulder he said, "Say, Chili. I hear you're cooking Sunday dinner. Now that you got yourself a fancy house, I imagine that'll get to be a family tradition. You coming, Jackson?"

She hadn't meant to scare him, but when he hurried out onto the veranda, Margo saw Ry's eyes were wide and searching.

"I'm here," she called out from her seat on the swing. She should have been tired, she should have felt the need to sleep the morning away, but instead she'd risen by seven, put on one of Ry's shirts and slipped out into the backyard to enjoy the morning jasmine.

"Don't do that," he scolded.

"Do what?"

"Disappear without telling me where you're going."

"I'm sorry. I couldn't sleep."

He stepped off the veranda, barefoot and shirtless, his jeans hugging his hips. He'd been awfully quiet driving home from the precinct. And when he'd made love to her, he'd been so serious, so possessive, that she'd suspected something was wrong. But she hadn't asked, sensing Ry would tell her soon enough. Now that everything was over, life would either go back to the way it was or..."

"We've got to talk." He sat down beside her.

"I'm listening."

He started rocking the swing. "A couple of those families had rewards out for their kids. The Chief told me Blu will receive several thousand dollars. It should help him get out of debt and put the fleet on its feet."

Margo was surprised. "Does he know?"

"He will soon enough. One of those kids was the daughter of a high-profile lawyer out east. He's requested a private meeting with Blu to discuss his future."

"Blu's future is the fishing fleet."

"Maybe." Ry stopped the swing to gaze down at her. "What's your plan for the future, baby?"

"I don't understand the question."

"I believe Koch is dead, but I'm still a cop and I'm still twelve years older than you are. It looks like you're the one with the decision to make."

Margo got to her feet and placed her hands on her hips. "So I get to do whatever I want, is that it?"

He hesitated. "That's the way it should work."

"Should?"

"Margo, I—"

"I love you, Ry Archard. I have since the day you walked into that alley and scared Jimmy Tandino into next week. I fell in love with Ryland, the man, but I also fell in love with who he was, a good cop. The best cop in New Orleans. I accepted that then, and I accept that now—the danger, the rotten schedule, the mood swings that a man in your business deals with."

"Margo—"

"I'm not finished," she insisted. "A few days ago I told you that I didn't believe in the justice system. But that wasn't true. I was just protecting myself, trying to fight the love I've had for you since I laid eyes on you at age fifteen. The news flash, Detective Archard, is that the attraction is burning hotter and brighter the older I get." Margo smiled. "Can you imagine how hot I'll burn when I'm eighty?"

"God, I love you."

"Then can we repaint the kitchen?" Margo teased.

Slowly Ry came to his feet. "Any color you wish."

He took a step forward. She took a step back.

"Stand still."

"Say it. Say it's forever this time."

"It would be my pleasure to make it forever this time, baby. Forever and legal. We'll call your mother and tell her there's going to be an afternoon wedding next Sunday in our backyard. A garden wedding."

He took another step forward, and this time Margo didn't move. "You're serious?"

"It's the only way I'm going to get you to stay home at least part-time and fill this house with beds and kids, right?"

"Children need parents. Married parents would make Mama happy."

"Come here."

Margo stepped into his arms, and he closed them around her. "It's going to be a wonderful life, Ry."

"Let me show you how wonderful."

"Right here?"

"Right here."

"You're a dirty old man, Ry."

"And you love me, anyway."

"Yes, I do."

****

Look out for Wendy Rosnau's next book,
Beneath the Silk, *in February 2004*
from Silhouette Sensation.

SILHOUETTE®
SENSATION™

AVAILABLE FROM 19TH DECEMBER 2003

LETTERS TO KELLY Suzanne Brockmann

When Jax Winchester was imprisoned on a trumped-up charge, only h
memories of Kelly O'Brien kept him going. But even after his release
couldn't truly be free until he'd kept his promise and claimed Kelly as
own…

IN THE LINE OF FIRE Beverly Bird

The Country Club
Ex-mobster Danny Gates and policewoman Molly French were unlike
allies. But when Molly uncovered a conspiracy behind the Country Cl
bombing, Danny was the only one she could trust. Could they uncove
the truth before their attraction got them both into trouble?

ALIAS SMITH AND JONES Kylie Brant

The Tremaine Tradition
When Analiese Tremaine chartered a boat to a remote island to find
brother, she was hiding her identity from its sexy captain, Jones—and
there was plenty he wasn't telling her. But reeling from his devastatin
kisses, could she rely on him to rescue her when she got into deep wa

WILDER DAYS Linda Winstead Jones

Somehow Victoria Lowell had got caught up in ex-love and undercov
agent Des Wilder's escape from a drug cartel. As they ran for their li
Victoria ached to uncover this man's secrets. But what would happer
when he discovered the truth about her child?

SMOKE AND MIRRORS Jenna Mills

When undercover cop Cassidy Blake infiltrated mercenary millionai
Derek Mansfield's life she expected to find a ruthless criminal. Inste
she found a man whose bone-melting intensity blurred the lines betw
her duty and desire. Could she risk her heart in this perilous game?

ON THIN ICE Debra Lee Brown

Seth Adams was working undercover to catch a corporate thief and v
back his FBI job. But Seth hadn't counted on falling for his prime
suspect, Lauren. Instinct told him she was innocent, but as the dang
escalated could Seth win the race against time to keep them alive?

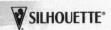

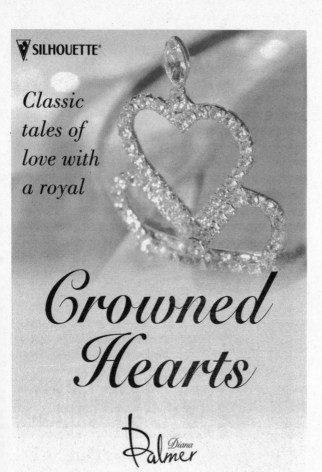

SILHOUETTE® SENSATION™

*proudly presents
a brand-new series from*

KYLIE BRANT

THE TREMAINE TRADITION

**Where undercover assignments lead
to unexpected pleasures...**

Alias Smith and Jones

January 2004

Entrapment

April 2004

Truth or Lies

July 2004

*Look out for more from Kylie Brant.
Coming soon!*

0104/SH/LC79

FREE

4 BOOKS
AND A SURPRISE GIFT!

We would like to take this opportunity to thank you for reading this Silhouette® book ▓ offering you the chance to take FOUR more specially selected titles from the Sensation™ seri▓ absolutely FREE! We're also making this offer to introduce you to the benefits of t▓ Reader Service™ —

★ FREE home delivery
★ FREE monthly Newsletter
★ FREE gifts and competitions
★ Exclusive Reader Service discount
★ Books available before they're in the shops

Accepting these FREE books and gift places you under no obligation to buy; you may cancel ▓ any time, even after receiving your free shipment. Simply complete your details below a▓ return the entire page to the address below. **You don't even need a stamp!**

YES! Please send me 4 free Sensation books and a surprise gift. I understand that unle▓ you hear from me, I will receive 6 superb new titles every month for just £2.90 eac▓ postage and packing free. I am under no obligation to purchase any books and may cancel ▓ subscription at any time. The free books and gift will be mine to keep in any case.

S3ZE▓

Ms/Mrs/Miss/Mr ....Initials................................

BLOCK CAPITALS PLE▓

Surname..

Address..

....

....Postcode ....

Send this whole page to:
UK: FREEPOST CN81, Croydon, CR9 3WZ
EIRE: PO Box 4546, Kilcock, County Kildare (stamp required)

Offer valid in UK and Eire only and not available to current Reader Service subscribers to this series. We reserve the right▓ refuse an application and applicants must be aged 18 years or over. Only one application per household. Terms and pri▓ subject to change without notice. Offer expires 31st March 2004. As a result of this application, you may receive offers fr▓ Harlequin Mills & Boon and other carefully selected companies. If you would prefer not to share in this opportunity please write▓ The Data Manager at the address above.

Silhouette® is a registered trademark used under licence.
Sensation™ is being used as a trademark.